Freak BOY

KRISTIN ELIZABETH CLARK

SQUARE
FISH

Farrar Straus Giroux

New York

SQUARE
FISH

An imprint of Macmillan Publishing Group, LLC
175 Fifth Avenue
New York, NY 10010
fiercereads.com

Square Fish and the Square Fish logo are trademarks of Macmillan and
are used by Farrar Straus Giroux under license from Macmillan.

Our books may be purchased in bulk for promotional, educational, or business use.
Please contact your local bookseller or the Macmillan Corporate and Premium
Sales Department at (800) 221-7945 ext. 5442 or by e-mail at
MacmillanSpecialMarkets@macmillan.com.

Library of Congress Cataloging-in-Publication Data
Clark, Kristin.
   Freakboy / Kristin Clark.
      pages   cm
   Summary: Told from three viewpoints, seventeen-year-old Brendan, a wrestler,
struggles to come to terms with his place on the transgender spectrum while Vanessa,
the girl he loves, and Angel, a transgender acquaintance, try to help.
   ISBN 978-1-250-06295-6 (paperback)   ISBN 978-0-374-32473-5 (ebook)
   [1. Novels in verse.   2. Sexual orientation—Fiction.   3. Transgender people—
Fiction.   4. High schools—Fiction.   5. Schools—Fiction.   6. Wrestling—Fiction.
7. Family life—Fiction.]   I. Title.

PZ7.5.C52Fre 2013
[Fic]—dc23

                                                                      2012050407

Originally published in the United States by Farrar Straus Giroux
First Square Fish Edition: 2016
Book designed by Colleen AF Venable
Square Fish logo designed by Filomena Tuosto

1   3   5   7   9   10   8   6   4   2

AR: 4.6 / LEXILE: HL700L

To every Freakboy and Freakgirl out there:

You are not a freak.

And you are not alone.

Author's Note

There are as many expressions of gender identity as there are individuals. No two are exactly the same. I would never in a million years attempt to tell *the* transgender story. All I can do is tell *a* transgender story and cross my fingers that people will be interested enough to start asking their own questions.

It is my hopeful intention that this will lead to conversation that will in turn draw us all along the path to a greater understanding and acceptance of gender's vast and lovely variation.

Peace and Love,
Kristin Elizabeth Clark

Pronoun

A pronoun is a ghost
of who you really are
short
sharp
harsh

whispering its presence,
taunting your soul.

In you
of you
but not
all you.

Struggling,
my own
He She
Him Her
I You.

Scared that
for scrambled-pronoun
Me,

We
might never
exist.

The Name Is Brendan
Dinner table,
silverware gleaming.
Claude the Interloper finishes
telling a story.

Mom passes me steak.

"How was your day?"

She's chirping, despite
surgery two days ago.

I shrug
the missed bus,
shrug
the half-hour wait for the next one,
shrug
the wrestling practice that blew.

Don't bother to elaborate.
Mom hates Coach
(almost) as much as I do.

Freshman year
she wanted me to skip holiday practice
so what was left of our family
could go on vacation.

Coach described the importance of
"consistent training and conditioning."
Said he always mentioned "dedication"
in his college letters of recommendation.

She wavered and then

he told her flat out that
I was the weakest link
and always would be if I was a
mama's boy who'd miss training.

She was ticked, but
we stayed in town
with the other manly
and dedicated jocks.

He was on my ass today
for getting caught
by a head-and-arm drag.
A crappy thing itself,
our faces so close.

Still he yelled.

And through all the drills
my head wasn't in it.

Wrestling Didn't Always Suck

Miller Prep Academy
requires a six-term
commitment to
at least one sport

and at first
it seemed like
less torture
than the others.

No ball to get nailed by,
or drop. No baton to fumble
in the last leg of the relay,
pissing off your teammates.

Just you and
your opponent.
Grappling
one on one.

But four years
of relentless splat on the mat have
brought out a bunch of little hells
I'd never even considered

so that now

I hate touching other guys.
I hate my own body.

And most of all?
I hate Coach Childers.

He calls me Brenda.

I Know What He's Saying

But I like girls. Always have,
even in elementary school.
Sandbox dust in my nose,
jungle gym–blistered hands.
Hanging with the guys,
but glad when a girl'd
ask me
      to
           play
                something.

Yeah, mostly the same games
when it came to
handball and foursquare.
But comfortable.
When you got hurt
girls'd ask
      what
          was
              wrong.

Guys would ignore you,
call you names
when your eyes watered
at the pop of a soccer ball to your face.

If you couldn't stop the tears
they'd yank out more words,
like "crybaby" (or worse), to
      hit

          you

              with.

And I loved the way girls wore their hair.
Ponytails bouncing, braids smooth.

Loved the colors they strutted
across the yard: bright purple, pink.

Loved other things they played,
like animal hospital or house.

Loved the sound of their voices
when

      they'd

         call

            to

me.

                              Still,

a shadow lurks
near the
edge
        of
                my
                        head
whispering,

"You like girls too much,

and not in
the same
        way
                everyone
                                else
does."

My Brain Takes Me Freaky Places

I twitch, gulp milk,
slam the glass back on the table.

A salad plate jumps.
Claude the Interloper frowns.
Mom winces.
Sister giggles.

"Hey, squirt," I say,
pinning girl-thoughts
to the mat and
gaining control
of my brain.

          "Do you like my princess hat?"

She tilts her head toward me
like I might not otherwise
notice the pink cone,
its lace ribbon dangling
close to her mac and cheese.

I move the plate a little.
"So you're a princess now."

          "No, Brendy, it's just
          for Halloween!"

A gap   toothed smile.

I was twelve
when she was born.
Everyone said we looked alike.
Mom's gray-blue eyes,
Dad's cheekbones.

But Courtney has it all over me
in the hair department—
hers thick, wavy, and long.
Mine straight, short, and,
I swear, already falling out.

Still, she's my favorite person
besides my girlfriend, Vanessa.
(Sounds lame, I know.)

I'm not religious; in fact
I'm not sure I even believe in God
        (though we used to go
            to church religiously [ha]),
but from the second Dad
put her
into my arms,
burrito-wrapped
in a little pink blanket,
innocent face
and tiny fingernails,
I saw Divine
attention to detail.
So small.

So perfect.

It's not a guy thing,
but I like babysitting.

Andy called her chick bait.
We used to push her stroller
to the park
and girls would wander over
to oooh
to ahhh.

When Courtney
took her first steps
toward me
Dad called me smitten.
Mom called me Little Mother.

That homey scene in eighth grade,
on my baby sister's first birthday.

Exactly one month before
Mom, the harp player, left
Dad, the biomedical engineer, for
Claude, the Interloper.

Conductor of San Diego Philharmonic.
His orchestra's music
poison to my father's ear.
Dad's banished—2,000 miles away.

(Not that we hung out a ton
when he lived closer
but at least it was an option.)

Now he's president of a biotech firm,
seen only in summer
when Mom needs to dump us—
        "Thanks, James! Ta-ta!!!"—
so she can tour with
her new   (and improved)
husband.

        "Big plans tomorrow?"
        she asks.

"Party at Andy's."

        Claude the Interloper
        raises an eyebrow.

He doesn't like Andy,
hates the way he just walks
into the house without knocking.

Thinks it's rude that Andy
checks out the food in our kitchen
when he's hungry
and maybe it is—

but I do the same thing at his house

and have since seventh grade,
a year before any of us were aware
of the Interloper's sorry existence.

> "I wanted to ask if you'd
> take Courtney
> trick-or-treating first."

Don't mind the trick-or-treating
but I'm tortured by the reason
Mom's asking.

She's recovering from
"an enhancement procedure"
and SURPRISE she's sore.

Still, I avert my eyes
from her new shape
and nod yes.

> "What are you going to be?"
> Court asks.

Now there's a question

and a depressing memory.

The Night I Was a Girl

Last year sucked.
The whole wrestling team
went to school as cheerleaders.
No choice but to go along.

Shaved legs and everything,
we all did it—even Rudy and Gil.

They're team co-captains.
Jerk-asses, towel snappers,
the first to bend fingers
when the ref's on the blind side.

They told Vanessa,
"Brenda looks so natural
she must do this a lot."

(Angel Hansted)

Opportunity Knocks
The bus makes a lurching turn
and I'm tellin' you,
I'm thrown against
the hottest guy ever
to wear a Halloween-theme tie.

He has that slicked-back,
butter-on-hot-corn-wouldn't-melt-
in-my-mouth, don't-touch-me-I'm-cool
look–but doesn't lean away
          not   at   first.

I can tell he's checking me out
but isn't gonna be obvious.
What's the point in being so shy, I
wanna ask him.   Get bold.

"Opportunity curves"
is what I say instead. He grins at me
for a second–then eyebrows raise.
He gets up and changes seats.

The smile
(it wasn't so
hot after all)
leaves when he clocks me.

I mostly pass–but
I've been made enough times to
know the exact second it happens.
And I just wanna say to Mr. Corn-hole
mouth,   "Your loss."

My stop's next, anyway.
Toss my head, get off
at Evergreen Community College.
Got my GED here.

I tell you now
classes are a habit.

Finish my degree
(social work major),
then it's off to difference-making
full-time employment
for Angel.

Maybe I can change up some things.
Someone's gotta do it.
Someone like me, I mean.
Someone who knows simple basics.

You wanna assign roommates
in group homes based on birth sex assignment?

Go ahead, idiot.
Make it easy for thugs to

S m e a r

the Queer.

Three Years Ago

My first day at Evergreen
I was ready for flight OR fight.
Out of the baking August parking lot
and into Admissions. I tell you—
my foster mom hadn't of been there
I mighta shot back through the door
like some kind of Olympic runner.

Stood at the end of the line,
freezing in my fuchsia tank top,
turquoise skirt, strappy gold sandals.

Girl, that building was icy but
the papers I held were floppy,
my hands sweatin' so bad.

Finally my turn. Big crabby-looking guy
with beady eyes called, "Next."
I went up to his window,
handed him my application.
He looked it over, looked at me,
and he
frowned.

People get uptight
when your ID
calls out a gender
different than what you present.

My foster mom touched my elbow
soft – lettin' me know she was there.

Still, my back was up when
Beady Eyes stepped away
to get a supervisor, muttering,

      "Right name, wrong gender."

And I'd heard it before–
but God was with me that day.

Beady Eyes's supervisor
came to the window.

      "You're Angel?" Adjusted her
      glasses. Looked over them.

      At me.

I nodded,
stretched my neck,
made sure my
courtesy-of-a-sadistic-
pervert-john
collarbone scars
showed.

Not afraid of *this*.
Ready to lay me down some attitude.

"We're admitting you today
but you might want
to get new state identification.

"You need a note
from your doctor and
signed by a witness,
the identification you have now,
and a special form, DL 328.

"Then your information
will match you better."

That sweet little old lady
winked at me
and I almost fell over.

Now every time
I pull out my ID
F for Female
feels like *T* for Triumph.

(Vanessa Girard)

In Ceramics
Hip against a metal plate,
the kickwheel squeaks
getting up to speed.

My hands slick the clay lump in front of me.

breathe   focus   center

      "It's art, Vanessa, not a competition,"
      the teacher, Mr. Mathews, says.

That doesn't keep him
from entering my pieces
in juried shows.
Contests they win

and I'm not going to lie—I'm proud

because I know
it isn't luck
or even talent
that takes first place.

It's practice and work
and the fact that
I stick with things
              even when they're hard.

Centering the Clay

takes concentration

Difficult

when one of your
two best friends
is standing by,
pestering you.

> "You're breaking
> Halloween tradition!"
> Julie's practically whining.

"We're too old for trick-or-treating," I tell her.

> Centering
> Centering
> Centering

> "C'mon, it'll be fun. Please?
> Two blind mice doesn't make sense."

Julie, Tanya, and I
have always
coordinated costumes.

When we were younger,
the three little pigs,
the three bears.

In high school we evolved.
Charlie's Angels,
the Three Musketeers.

Now we're regressing to the three blind mice?

"Sorry—I promised Brendan
I'd go to Andy's party."

And I'm not telling her but
I already bought my costume:
ooh la la, French maid.

Sexier than a hooded sweatshirt,
sunglasses, and a rope tail for sure.

Julie rolls her eyes.
"Of course you promised *Brendan*—I
guess we'll do something else."

Centering.
Centering.
Centering.

"Meet us at Andy's?"
The invite for show—out of guilt
because if all works out
we won't be there for very long.

The clay
on the wheel goes
a little   side
ways.

"Whatever." She's
already turning away.

"We'll see."

At Home with Trick-or-Treaters at the Door

I grab keys to the Beamer,
hoping to escape while
Mom gives Snickers
to a warlock and a ninja.

She shouldn't get a good look
at what I'm wearing.
Her fashion sense
is more L.L.Bean than Ooh La La.

(And for some crazy reason
my dad doesn't seem to mind.
So much for the widely touted
French sense of style—
I'd say he just left it behind
when he moved to the U.S.
but somehow he's managed
to keep it for himself.)

"Not too late!" Mom calls.

Pretending not to hear
is what I do best.

I'm picking up Brendan
and even though we've been together a long time
my rib cage has that great fizzy, funny feeling.

I've liked him since
I was a freshman.

He's a year older—and the only wrestler
who was nice to me when I joined the team.

I've loved him since
I was a sophomore.

I got my license that September—
wasn't supposed to drive
anyone else for six months.

Oops.

Two weeks after I got it
I saw Brendan hunching
toward the bus stop,
his Miller Prep uniform
damp with October rain.

I offered him a ride.

We got to his house,
sat in the car for another hour
talking about

everything.

He called when I got home
and we talked for three more.

He knows my secrets.

(When we visit my father's family in Cannes
I'm embarrassed for my mom.
My *tantes élégantes* talk about her in French
she doesn't understand.
I do, but don't defend her.)

I know his deep darks, too.

(He got superlethargic
when his parents split up.
Wouldn't get out of bed
on the weekends.
His mom thought he just
needed time to adjust.

His dad and the court disagreed.
Brendan's bitter about the compromise:
custody for Mom, Zoloft for him.)

For three weeks
we were just friends
until the night
of the crazy windstorm.

He was babysitting Courtney.
I stopped by to say hi

and she'd just gone to sleep
in spite of the wail
of a seventy-mile-an-hour wind
that snapped power lines

and slammed
Southern California
into darkness.

He got out flashlights   lit candles.

Our hands made
shadow puppets
on the wall.

First fingertip kisses   then lips.

The Santa Ana Wind
gusts down
desert canyons.

Hot. Dry. Electric.

Some say
it ignites tempers.

I say
it ignited us.

It howled around outside,
battering the house
with dried palm fronds.

Debris snatched up
flung down
snatched up again.

A wind so greedy
it couldn't bear
to discard the tiniest scrap.

A greedy wind that wanted it all.

And when

our lips touched
for the first time

I flamed up
greedy too

and the pounding in my ears
could have been
the rush of my blood

or the Santa Ana wind
shrieking
for more.

A Year Later

we still
remind
each other
of that
first kiss.

"It's windy,"
I'll say
every time
he comes up
behind me,
lifts my hair
off my neck,
gently blows
just behind
my earlobe.

"It's windy,"
he'll whisper,
arms wrapped around me.

And I'm still greedy. Greedier, in fact.
We've talked about it—
kissing's not enough anymore.

We haven't discussed specifics, like
exactly when or where,
but I have a few ideas.
So, Mom?
           Tonight I could be home late.

How Do You Know When the Time Is Right?

(A) When you're in love?
(B) When your body aches for something more?
(C) When you've both decided you're ready?
(D) All of the above?

Hope my drive-your-man-crazy costume
keeps its promise.

In wrestling I'm hot
and sweaty
like the guys.
So off the mat,
I admit I tend to go
girly overboard.

But is it enough?

When I get to his house
he slumps into the car
and I taste his funky mood
in our kiss.

"You didn't dress up."
Like he needs me
to point it out.

"There's no law," he says.

"But it'd be fun, right?
Last year you looked so cute!"

  "Last year sucked."
  His flat voice shuts me out.
  "Besides, I didn't have time.
  I had to take Courtney out."

Moody Brendan's in the house.

  "What kind of a mother
  schedules a boob job three days
  before Halloween?"

"One with small tits?" I ask,
hoping for a smile that doesn't come

but he does reach over,
rest his hand on my leg.

I start the car.
We drive a block.
Then two.
Then three.

"C'mon—what's wrong?"

  "Halloween's just
  not my thing."

"So *that's* why
you didn't
mention my costume!"
I'm trying for flirty, and

                    he looks over.
                    "Nice."

But there's no smile.
And it's no use.
I turn the corner,

a deflated French maid
in fishnet stockings
and a short skirt.

(E) Quiz postponed.

Gloom Seeps Over Different Expectations

Andy's house, a parent-free zone tonight.
Light spills out the open front door—
party's on downstairs,
upstairs windows are   b l a c k.

I park the car. Brendan
sits, doesn't get out.
I love him but know
there's no way to rescue his   m o o d.

If that were possible, I'd go in,
say hi, steal beer, and park
somewhere—talk, laugh, kiss.
Whatever it   t o o k.

He's complicated. Sometimes
just shy. Antisocial. Or
depressed. And I'm okay
when it's only   u s.

Tonight the situation sucks.
I blew off fun with my best friends
to be with Brendan. I'd do it again but sometimes
I wish there was a way to be with   b o t h.

Still, if it came right down to it?
A forever choice?
I'd choose him.
Always.

Some Truths Don't Go Over So Well

Especially not with friends
you've had since fifth grade.

This past summer Julie and Tanya bitched
I never spent time with them,
but that wasn't true.

We hung out a lot
when Brendan went away
to see his dad.

But when I pointed that out,
Tanya said it didn't count.

And even though I DID
invite them to this party,
I know they're mad at me
for ditching our
trick-or-treat tradition.

They just don't understand—

Julie's never been serious about a guy
and Tanya's never had a boyfriend at all.

I can't help it if
I'd rather be with him
than anyone else.

That's love.

(BRENDAN)

Last Night's Mistake
Throbbing music.
Throbbing bodies.
Throbbing headache this morning.

Wish we'd just gone in,
said hi, stolen beer,
parked somewhere.

But Vanessa wanted to party.
And I knew I wasn't good company.

Barely over the threshold,
it was Andy.
            "You fag, you didn't dress up!"
            Loud over booming bass.
"Good to see you, too."
He couldn't hear me.
Instead, he handed me
a half-empty
bottle of Jack and then
pulled on his hockey mask.
            "Dude, we're going
            to the graveyard!
            We're going to
            have a séance
            for Mr. Fredricks!"
Like this was a good idea?
Slasher movies aside,

didn't he think
kids + Halloween + graveyard =
trouble of the police variety?

But how can someone who
doesn't speak up
be the voice of reason?
So I went along
with the crowd.

Bottle concealed
under my sweatshirt,
Vanessa at my side.

Trick-or-treaters were
home by that time,
counting their loot
or in bed already

and the two blocks
of asphalt
between Andy's house
and that of the dead
were empty.

Except for the fifteen or so of us,
a small mob of pirates, witches,
ghosts, and zombies, like something
out of the Charlie Brown
Halloween special.

The foggy mist felt
good on my skin
and oddly enough
(while heading to a cemetery)
my mood started to get better.

Over the wrought iron fence,
we scattered apart
in and around
the stone garden.

I pulled Vanessa along
with one hand,
held the bottle
with the other,
and tried to keep up with Andy
weaving between headstones and
jog-walking past the mausoleum.

Mr. Fredricks, the choir director,
had a heart attack my freshman year.
Now his grave's like
a Halloween tourist attraction.

He's buried in the corner
farthest from the road,
relatively safe
from a getting-in-trouble
standpoint.

Me and Andy and Vanessa
were the first to get there,
I thought. We stood, staring
at his name carved
on a metal-plated block.

"Alas, poor Fredricks,
I knew him well," I said.

It wasn't true
though he'd always been
nice to me, considering
I couldn't sing.

I was just
taking off
on a line from *Hamlet*,
required reading senior year.

A swig from the bottle.
Then Gil jumped out from
behind a nearby tombstone.

And even though I'd expected
something like it somewhere
in the back of my head,
my heart slammed
into my throat
and I yelled.

"You scream like a girl!"
First Gil was laughing,
then Andy joined in.
"Screw you," I said,
trying to sound jokey.
(At least Vanessa didn't laugh.)
Gil's eyes narrowed.
"What did you say?"
"Aw, c'mon."
Tried to keep it light.
Gil's an eighty-two-pounder—

wrestle-speak for
one hundred eighty-two.

Big.

A wild man
on the mat.
Off the mat
just a dirty fighter.

"I didn't scream like a girl."
My vocal cords wispy,
traitorous.

Andy pointed to Fredricks's grave.
"Look, I see a ghost!"
Distracting Gil,
the ugly drunk.

I'm always
a little surprised
when
Andy
has my back.

He howled
and pretty soon
from distant places
other kids, other voices
joined in.

"Woooo wooooo."

Until the wailing
was joined by a different kind.
Cemetery neighbors
probably called the police.

Flashing lights at the front gates
gave just enough time
for us to jump the fence,
    s c a t t e r   laughing   g a s p i n g,

back to the house
where Gil forgot to punch me

or maybe he just didn't want
to risk a fight with Andy
who's even bigger than him
and a black belt, too.

Everyone else partied,
breathless enthusiasm over
the graveyard adventure,

while my ears flamed
at the memory of
my voice
my shriek
my girlish
noise.

I pushed Vanessa
to dance in the crush of bodies,

       (why should she suffer
       just because I was miserable?)

I stood to the side.

And drank.
And watched
my beautiful
girlfriend.

And waited

to go home.

Where

      thanks to a mom
      who never waits up
      even when she's
      not recovering
      from surgery

I could be
all by
my
ugly

               self.

After Vanessa Dropped Me Off

I crashed in bed
but lay awake forever
            hearing my girl-voice, Gil's laugh.

Reliving the shittiness
through the hours
until finally I drowsed

into that dream I've had
off and on
since freshman year,

more
often
lately.

            And if the dream
            itself isn't
            bad enough

            the way I always feel
            when I wake up
            is worse,

            sense-memories
            that make me sweat
            like I just got off the mat.

Nightmare

Courtney clenched in a dragon's fist.
I stand below,
arms stretched out

worried.

I sacrifice myself to save her
by turning into a hot princess
while everyone else looks

confused.

I'm dragon bait,
still I feel right
with full breasts, long hair—

peaceful.

I wake up
to flat chest,
morning wood,

nauseous.

Thank God for Dry Toast

I gnaw, trying to focus
on that instead of my dream
or how shitty I feel.

Trying to focus on the fact
I have to make it through
wrestling during the
stupid-early
zero period
before school starts,
then class
and a test in AP Calculus
(easy if only I wasn't hungover).

A sick-the-day-after-
Halloween story and
Coach'd pour on the abuse.

Brush my teeth,
shove my feet
into shoes
I don't bother to tie.

No one awake to
shout bye to.
I finally drag my body
onto the 34 West bus.

Too early for crazies
except me
who dreams of
turning into a girl.

And likes that feeling.
Does that make me gay?

Alone in my weirdness,
buildings (filled with normal people)
swirl past; my stomach bubbles.

My forehead's slick
against the seat
in front of me.

A groan escapes.

Across the aisle
a real girl speaks up.
My true self
must not show.
                    "Big night?" she asks.

Can't tell if she's making fun,
risk nodding yes,
avert my eyes—

in case
they really

are a window
into my twisted soul.

"You okay?"

What can you say to that?
I mean, with honesty.
Nothing.

"I'm fine."

But in the next second
I know I'm going to puke
if I don't get off.

Right now.

Just then she pulls the cord,
the bus glides to a stop. Thank God.
I stumble off, reach a
sidewalk planter just in time.

After the dry toast
and last night's Jack is gone
(no trouble making weight today)
I feel better—except the
girl from the bus stands
holding out a water bottle.

I shake my head.

No candy from strangers.

> "Someone had too much
> fun last night, for sure!"
> Offers the bottle again.
> "Never been opened."

"No thanks." Why is she being so nice?

> "No rinse?" she asks.

"I'm okay." Now I really
can't look her in the eye.

> "Suit yourself," she says
> but she doesn't sound mad.
> "I work right here."

> Points to the building whose
> shrubs I just baptized with my
> breakfast, all hail the holy vomit.

"Sorry."

Please God, just send
another bus now.

> "It's okay.

> "Look, if you want to come in and
> get cleaned up, it's a teen center . . ."

Again I shake my head. A block away
the next bus rounds the corner. See?
Maybe God answers prayers.

(If you're careful not to ask for
anything that's not in his goodie bag—
apparently he mostly keeps stuff like
salvation and plagues in there.)

    "Okay, okay," she says. She's
    smiling again.
    "But do me a favor—
    tie your shoes."

I feel like an idiot,
bend down to tie and that
makes my head pound again.
She puts the water back
in her purse, writes
something on a slip of paper.

    "If you ever want to talk . . ."

Older than me.
Twenty-something maybe?

Flirting? Or just being friendly?

I take the paper,
purple sparkly ink
spells out *Angel Hansted*,
her phone number,
then underneath,
Willows Teen Center.

The bus stops.
Muscles tense,
I say thanks, board,
shove her note into my backpack,
take a seat, look out the window,
see her stride toward the building.

Tall,
graceful,
easy in her skin.
She's hot.

See? I'm not gay.

(Angel)

Off the Bus
and at Willows Teen LGBTQ Center
ass-crack-of-dawn early.
I left my music theory book
here last night. I'll pick it up,
come back to open the doors
after class.

Kids'll straggle in later. Just like
I used to: ditching school, foster care,
parents, assholes who mistreat them.

They'll hang out in the rec room.
Faded couches, torn-up magazines,
a big TV.
Laughing, bickering, gossiping.
Being themselves.

Waiting for Group with Dr. Martina
or afternoon classes,
learning everything from how to
avoid date rape to
balancing a checkbook,

and if donors have been
generous with supplies,
a little underwater basket weaving
thrown in there, too.

When I'm Not at School
I'm hanging at the center.
Part-time receptionist,
crafts leader,
janitor.

My friends don't get why
I'm here so much.

> "No offense, Girl–
> you a glutton for
> punishment!
> Everybody there
> look so sorry–
> and you *a i n' t.*"

Meant as a compliment, but see–
kids at the center? Not just sorry;
sad sometimes; scared, f yeah–and if
they're sorry it's not what
the girlfriend means by *s o r r y.*

When it comes to the ones I
hang with, even the ones who at least
got their shit together enough to find
their way here, the kind of sorry *I' m*

talking about is just the sorry that
they are who they are. In the world
that hurts us all, even *m e.*

The Bus Roars Away
and I wonder about the kid.
Hungover, twitchy, uncomfortable, lost.

Familiar.

Those untied shoes reminded
me of my little brother.
Frankie never tied his either.

I unlock Willows
and walk around
the front desk.

Jim from Adult Day Care
shuffles in.
Supposed to be next door.

     "Got any beer, Girlie?"
     Same question every time.

We're some distant-memory
liquor store in his brain.

"Nuh-uh, Jim, time to go back."
I grab my book, take his elbow,
lock up again.

Deliver him to a nurse–
his keeper of the day.

"Second time this week,"
I tell her.

Her skinny face gets red like
I'm blaming her for his escape.
(Oooh, that's right, I am.)

She takes him by the sleeve.
"Come sit down," she tells him.
"You just got confused."

Glares at me.
"Everybody does,
sometime or other."

Confused? Hardly.

I'm twenty years old and I never been
confused a day in my life.

Grew up in a white neighborhood
till I was fourteen. Mexican mama and all.

She met my dad working
in the clean room for his company.
Had to wear one of those ugly
white spaceman outfits they have
so dust doesn't get in
the computer chips.

He must of liked what he saw
when she took off her helmet,
shook her thick hair, because
Smooth Dude swept Cinderella off
to a gated community in La Jolla.

Mama hated it. Hated living there—
said she had more in common
with the pool man than
with the white neighbor ladies.

"It's not real," she'd tell me and Frankie,
about that difference we couldn't hide.
"But they think it is."

The bigger difference
I couldn't hide
      even back then
caused a giant shit-storm.

In kindergarten she had to pick me up.
Baby Frankie, nap interrupted,
suckin' his thumb in the car seat.

Mama's knuckles, copper metal
crunching the steering wheel.

      "Angel, you HAVE to stay out
      of the girls' bathroom!"

The third time.
In three days.

"There's BOYS in the other one!"
Thinking she HAD to understand,
but Mama shook her head.

      "If you can't use the right one,
      you better hold it
      till you get home."

I couldn't use the right one
'cause they wouldn't let me.
Was it my fault they couldn't see
who I was? Nope.

None of this
"trapped-in-a-man's-body" bullshit.

I am a woman.
And back then?

I was a little girl.

I Like a Challenge
I'd have to, right?
Getting ground into
the mat six days a week.

My mom's proud of what she
calls my competitive spirit,
no matter what form it takes.

Dad's side of the family?
A different story
though it's really their fault.

Spring break in France
every year since I was born.
Three cousins my age. All boys.

Charles, Étienne, Gaston:
smug, superior, cliquish
always a contest with them—

run faster
hold your breath longer
find more Easter eggs.

Subdue your partner
pin him to the beach
smile when he gets mad.

We'd wrestle on the shore,
Greco-Roman rules, and I
learned to think two moves ahead.

Scrappy, with no bigger wish
than to triumph over them,
no sweeter joy than when I did.

Until I was twelve, that is. Grand-maman—
of the floppy hat and severe eyebrows—
ended it, calling me *fille d'une truie*,

daughter of a female pig.
The *tantes élégantes* laughed.
I pretended not to hear

and even nodded respectfully when
Grand-maman, perfumey hand on mine,
told me, *en français*, "No boy wants a rough girl."

I quit without a fight because
I was tired of sand that
clung to my scalp, stuck in my ears—

but I wasn't tired of wrestling. Winning.
And from the safe distance of La Jolla
I joined the team my freshman year.

It took a conference with
Miller Prep's headmaster,
my mom, Coach, the dean of students,
and the school psychologist
for me to even get to try out.

(It was helpful that the public school
down the street
had just settled a lawsuit by
Lenora Jenkins,
now their thirty-five-pounder.)

On the mat, my moves
spoke for themselves and
since then Coach
has had to admit
I'm an asset
to the team.

In the beginning

I got called dyke a lot
put up with bullshit from everyone
even some of my teammates.

Still, I win more than I lose.
I'm strong. And the best thing?
A "rough girl" got the boy,

Brendan.

A Change of Weather

This morning
humid rain,
car windows fog
with my breath,
hot coffee.

It's hard to see
the school parking lot
from this cocoon
but I hear vehicle doors slam,
remote locks beep.

I brought Brendan's favorite, mocha and a muffin.
Maybe I should have brought soda crackers;

he was pretty drunk
when I dropped him off
last night.

But oh, so sweet.

I drove with my left hand
while he held my right—

            "I love you so much." Rubbing my
            thumbnail
            over and over
            like I was his Aladdin's lamp.
            "You're the best."

Leaned his head against me—
"Sorry, so sorry about tonight."

I parked in front of his house.
He stroked my hair.
Played with it.
Kissed me.
Then got out
of the car
a little unsteady,
shut the door.

I rolled down
the passenger window
and he bent his head
to look at me.

"God, your costume is hot."

So What if Last Night Didn't Go as Planned?

Good things come
to those who wait.

This morning I got a call from
our neighbor two doors down.
The Smiths are going away for Thanksgiving
and need me to feed their cat.

They'll leave house keys in our mailbox.

The thought of a private place
just for me and Brendan
fills my chest
with a cozy something,
makes me smile.

I peer out the windshield again
sipping my latte and
wondering which Brendan
will show.

Don't get me wrong.
It's not like he's totally schizo—
but with him you can't
always predict who you'll get.

Sweet Brendan
Hilarious Brendan
Driven Brendan

Playful Brendan
Soulful Brendan

Distant Brendan

depending on the day, the mood.

Inside
and out
different
aspects

combine, make up the whole.

I love them all
because
I love him.

(BRENDAN)

Lucky

She waits   for me
Warm coffee   cold hands
First thing   I say
I know   I'm lucky

     And aren't I

Late night,   too tired
this morning   to think
Our kiss   feels good.

In the Gym

"Hello, ladies."
Coach's daily greeting
and he's not addressing Vanessa.

Partner up
spin drill, shoot the tube,
take down, hip heist, sprawl.

Tired.
Distracted.
Reeking.

The stink of
last night's Jack,
this morning's sweat

ignored by Coach when he demos
a punishing arm drag.
Hot breath in my face,
mat burn on my elbow,

a gasping glance
at the clock.
Caught.

"Quit being a pussy, Brenda."

Vanessa Snags My Water Bottle

After
wind sucking   sweat dripping
conditioning
hot room   close bodies

bad enough
she outwrestles me

it's worse when
Coach rides me
and I look like a loser.

So I have
a rule for us.
No contact.

Don't look   don't talk

In wrestling

you're not   my girlfriend

you're just one of the guys.

She goes along
but thinks it's stupid,
always makes a point
of catching my eye   holding it

and drinking my bottle dry.

At Home After Dinner

The Interloper and Courtney
go out for ice cream
and the soothing sound
of a harp glissando
battles thoughts
in my
propeller brain.

Mom's recovered enough
to lift her arms—
her music slides up
the staircase once again
the sound track to my homework.

Tomorrow I have
6 a.m. wrestling, AP Bio test,
quiz on the first act of *Hamlet*,
after-school conditioning,
endless homework.

Whirling brain gets stuck
on princess dream
and won't come loose
on girlfriend.

Not gay.
Then what?

Maybe lots of guys dream
of being turned into girls?
For some reason
I've never asked Dr. Andrews.

(He's not big on talk therapy.
Just the same questions.

    "Suicidal thoughts? Tendencies?
    No? Here's your scrip.")

Prescriber of Zoloft.
Reliever of paternal anxiety.

Dad:
    "Hey, buddy, you seem down,
    a doctor can help with that."

Fulfiller of court-ordered
maternal duty.

Mom:
    "I don't know if James thinks
    Brendan's really depressed, or if
    he's just trying to make things harder."

Voilà! My twice-yearly visit to the shrink
mollifies one and absolves the other.

Because my busy brain
uncertain moods
ulcerative anxiety
and general malaise
are my own fault.   Right?

I toss aside the calculator
and grab my MacBook,

(a bribe from
the Interloper)

Start to type
Dreams of being a girl.

My fingers hesitate,
I swallow.

Type
Want to be a girl
instead.

Links pop up
and I see the word

"transsexual."

When I Was a Little Kid
my dad gave me
a green plastic submarine.

It had a tiny compartment
that you'd shake baking soda
into—and that
made the thing
bob
and dive.

I'd play with it
for hours
wrinkled fingers
pruney palms.

Sometimes
I'd hold
the sub
underwater
thumb half covering
the topside hole,
watch baking soda fizz
to the surface
where
bubbles
would pop.

And if I held the
little hatch closed,

then let go of the toy,

the whole thing would
shoot out of the water.

Splash.

The prickle of feeling
I have when I wake
from a dream
of being in the right skin

of catching my reflection
in the mirror when
I've gone too long
without a haircut

of being into how that
softens the angle
of my jaw,
frames my face

like a girl's

those are fizzy bubbles

rising
on **THAT** word
up to the
top and
pop.

Thinking that being in love
with Vanessa
should have made it
all go away,

that's me
holding the submarine
deep
under
water—

compartment closed and

I don't want to let go.

Splash.

When That Word Bursts

up from the depths,
a drop of water
clings to it.

Small but visible

to my naked eye.

A tiny drop
to hold so much;

inside it is my princess dream.

And a horror that
    starts small,

multiplies

with other droplets containing
                drowsing sensations,
                    fleeting desires.

The water gathers until
    certain knowledge that this
        ugly word applies to me,
            becomes a tidal wave that

                    knocks me
                            over.

Transsexual

Snap
screen
shut.

Grab my bus pass,
charge downstairs.

I have to move
get out
get away.

Transsexual

"Going to the library,"
I shout toward the
music room's
closed door,
and then
I'm outside
running

Transsexual

past wide
lawns,
huge
Band-Aid-colored
stucco houses,
fake streams,
and fake waterfalls.

Transsexual

Skid to
the stop.

A bus pulls around
the corner and
I don't look at
which one it is
don't care
where it's headed.

I just need to
ride

Transsexual

for a long time.

When it
gets too quiet

the word
too loud.

Transsexual

I get off

at stops
        familiar
        unfamiliar.

Take the next one
that comes my way

zigzag across the city
and back.

TRANSSEXUAL

I stare
into the dark
until a guy
about my age
about my size,

gets on
grunts
across
the aisle.

Cigarette smell
bar code–tattooed neck
ring-pierced eyebrow
announce him.

He's Tough Guy.

And he's looking at me.   For a fight?

I turn my head

Transsexual

my face feels ugly
I make it uglier
just in case.

When the bus
stops I get off
on a dim street.

Am *I* looking for a fight?

Tough Guy
doesn't follow.

But my fists
don't unclench.

I *was* looking for a fight.

The bus heaves off
into the late night.

I turn around
and BAM

Willows Teen Center
looms   ahead
on the empty block.

I get closer, see the
smaller letters painted
on darkened windows.

A PLACE FOR LGBTQ YOUTH.

Transsexual

My heart slams
into my throat
exactly like that night
in the graveyard
but my stomach
is sick, too.

Is that why the girl
was so nice?
Did she think I was gay?

Is there something about me?
Something obvious
I don't recognize but
others do?

How can other people
see something in me
that I have never seen
in myself?

Transsexual

No breath
deserted block.

Transsexual

Next to the curb
a river stone
just bigger than
my fist.

Rounded, smooth,
like something
you'd see in the back
of a landscaper's truck
nestled with others
of its kind.

Transsexual

Here,
out of place,

                   lonely

in the middle
of the sidewalk.

Transsexual

My fingers close
around it

cool
to the touch

heavy
in my palm.

A current rushes
my body
shoots through
my arm,

a hand that isn't mine
hurls a rock
it wasn't holding

right through the
T for Teen Center

T for

Transsexual

Glass Shatters

shocks my ears
and I'm off
running
up the block
away from
here.

What the hell
what the Hell
what the HELL.

Alarms should
     be screaming.
Lights should
     be flashing.
People should
     be shouting.

But the street sleeps on.

I round the corner just
in time for the next bus.

It picks me up,
takes me toward home as if

everything
is   fine.

(Angel)

Sometimes the Real World Hurts

'Specially when you're looking
at it through a hole some
homophobic asshole made
by throwing shit
through the window
of a center for queer kids.

> Bus takes me by here
> on my way to the class
> I'm gonna miss
> 'cause this morning I got off
> to see why
> Dr. Martina
> and the PoPo were
> standing outside.

There's broken glass,
a rock
inside.

> Officer takes a report, then tells
> us catching someone probably
> won't happen. Dr. Martina nods,
> shrugs. "I figured."

Wait, we're just supposed
to lay down and take it?

"This stuff happens, Angel,"
she says to the face I'm pulling.

When the cop leaves I get out
the Shop-Vac. Doctor tapes the hole,
calls around for replacement glass.

This is so fucked up
I got the shakes
like a junkie.

"So there's nothin'
at all we can do,"
I say when she hangs up.

    "We *are* doing something.
    Every day we fight ignorance
    and hatred with education."

I like the good doctor too much
to tell her what bullshit
that sounds like right now

when I'm standing here
looking at all the shiny
pieces on the floor

and I'm thinking
of the glass coffee table
that broke
when
the Sperm Donor
pushed me into it.

How blood soaked
my favorite Juicy shirt.

> "No son of mine!"
> Damn straight–and now
> I'm not his daughter either.

I know Jesus says forgive but
I'm not Jesus–I'm just a girl with
a vacuum cleaner, suckin' up shards,

and they may look like they're gone
'cause you can't see 'em,
but they're poking around inside.

I Pray to God
and it's not just
for me I'm praying.

I think of the kids
coming in
seeing that taped-up window
hearing what happened.

Bad enough they get
told at home
at school
on the street
that they aren't okay.

A broken window
of the only place that
welcomes 'em

gives the message

there's not one single

                    spot

on this earth
that they are
safe.

(BRENDAN)

All the Next Day
the question I'm asking,
"What the hell?"
trails me.

And
that   other   word
follows it right behind.

Toilet paper
stuck to
my shoe.

What a crappy thing
to do.

What a crappy thing
to be.

All I need is
a bar code tattoo,
an eyebrow piercing,
and a sex change

to announce
to the world
I'm the new
American degenerate.

Freak-style.

Tuesday morning,
AP History,
looking for a pen
in my backpack

fingertips brush
the paper
that girl
gave me
outside of Willows.

*What did she see
when she looked at me?*

Guilty, I imagine
her kneeling,
picking up glass,
cutting herself.

thug
          thug
                    thug
                              thug
                                    thug

In class
out of class
wrestling practice
awkward ride home.

("Just in a bad mood,"
my excuse to Vanessa.)

Then finishing college applications
where the writing prompt asking me to
describe an incident that changed me
brings on a whole new anxiety.

Trans
            trans
                        trans
                                    trans
                                            trans
                                                    What

Transgender.
Transwoman.
Transformed into a freak.
Transported to hell.

A Couple Days Later

Andy comes over
after dinner.
We're headed upstairs
when Mom grabs me. Says,

     "You look tired."

I grunt.

     "Were you up late
     playing video games?"

"No."

     "Are your applications done?"

"Mostly."

I brush by her.
Andy's ahead of me
already disappearing
into my room.

I go after him, thinking
focusing on gaming's a good idea.

That escapist virtual world
trumps this one

with its
twisted question
electric in my brain:

WHAT IF IT'S TRUE?

College Applications, Round One

Most due Monday after Thanksgiving and
I've hit Send on a few already, like
my first choice, U of Chicago.

But what does it matter?

U of C or Berkeley,
good schools for math,
UW–Madison,

the school Andy's hoping for;
his whole family's gone there.

I glance over at him
hulking on the floor
next to my bed
controller in hand
playing an old-school game.

> "We could live together,"
> he says, eyes glued to the
> screen. "You'd bring the PS3,
> —I'd bring the Xbox.

> "We wouldn't have to worry
> about sharing a room
> with some weenie."

I want to pause Mortal Kombat
shout, puke, something—
the thought of rooming with anyone . . .

What if he knew
about trans-thuggy me?
What would he do?

I can't see
next year at all
and really,
why bother thinking ahead?

I'm a freak and my future
is   totally   screwed.

I take a shot,
push my kill streak to five,
lean back.

"Sounds good," I say.

And I'm sorry the game is over.

Wednesday After Conditioning

I hang around
outside the girls'
locker room.

I'm scrambled
strung out
scared but

missing Vanessa
adds to the
turmoil factory.

Lately it's mostly been
ILY texts between classes,
forbidden looks in wrestling,
lame excuses for taking the bus home.
It's felt too weird
I've felt too weird
for close contact

and now my arms
hurt with wanting
to hold her.

She finally appears,
fresh from the shower
damp hair in
a ponytail—
smiles to see me—but,

"I have to go to
the airport to
get Grand-maman."

"Paper to write," I say.

She leans in.
        "Thanksgiving night
        we'll have all the
        time in the world."
Her dark eyes are steady.

She's already told me
about the Smiths' empty house . . .

I don't look down
when her fingertip
brushes my chest.

There's no mistaking
exactly what
we'll have
all the time
in the world
to do.

I breathe her in,
        the wanting
                overpowers
                        the awkward.

Soft lips
touch mine
before
she walks
away

and
that word
gets quieter.

Vanessa has no idea
I'm a massively confused
vandalizing menace.

With her I'm
someone else
something else

and I can
grab that
feeling

hang on like
it's my opponent trying to
get out of a double arm bar.

Thanksgiving night
is the night.

(Angel)

Mama's Sweet Corn Stuffing
sits on the table; she'd be proud.
Turkey, sweet potato pie,
spaghetti, onion rings.

I check out the offerings
of my sisters-in-spirit,
Denai, Brandy, Chantal.
Not bad for a bunch of girls
(used to be) from the street.

Gennifer's not here
'cause she's spending the night
with her boyfriend–lucky.

But, Girl, we're lucky ones, too.

Roof over our heads, even if it's five
in a two-bedroom apartment
and seems like there's always
someone in the bathroom.

Legally employed . . . mostly.

Brandy sells a little pot,
adds to what she
gets as a telemarketer.
         She's saving for surgery.

We're lucky to be giving thanks
with the family we've chosen.

Show the world
your essence
and you find out
faster than a
five-dollar hand job
who's family
and who's not.

The ugly-ass
Sperm Donor
who beat the crap
out of you for
dressing like yourself?

A cracked rib
the least of the pain.

Who sent you to
"Hoods in the Woods"
after your mama died?
Thinking they'd teach you
how to be a man–

like learning to catch fish
and dig a latrine
to shit in
could change your DNA,
your soul.
Who You Are.

The asshole
who threatened
to call the police
after he threw you out
just 'cause you snuck back
to see your
baby brother

and the little guy used to
cry and beg for you to stay
because he lost his mother
and his sister the same year,
                    then he was the lost one?

No, the Sperm Donor
is NOT family.
I count my
blessings and
thank God.

It's the American Way
of an American holiday.

Mom jokes that my father and Uncle Michel
have embraced it too fully since
moving here twenty years ago.

Too much turkey, stuffing, gravy,
mashed potatoes, pumpkin pie.

Before they settle down
to snooze in front of the TV,
Dad waves me over to commence
the Thanksgiving ritual of gently rapping my leg
with his knuckles to hear if it's hollow.

> "Where does such a little girl
> hide so much food?" he asks,
> eyebrow cocked, fake puzzlement.

"I'm not telling you!" I play along, jerking away
while he tries to hang on and we tussle.

Yeah, it's dorky and we both know
I'm too old for the game—
but I think he thinks it's fun
to see the disapproval radiating
off Grand-maman.

"Lucas! She's a young lady,"
his mother scolds.

My father catches my eye,
winks, then shares a smirk
with Uncle Michel.

"Strange, no? A young lady
with a hollow leg she hides food in!"
My father gives me one last tickle.

I walk back into the kitchen
to tell Mom I'm going out
but she's already (discreetly)
headed upstairs
probably to escape Grand-maman,

who follows me, practically
catching me with her claws.

"Where is your young man?"

"Home.
I thought I'd go hang with him
for a couple hours."

"Let him come to you.
Men chase women, *chérie*,
this is the nice way.
They run from the ones
who get that wrong."

I nod (respectfully) and
sit down at the breakfast bar,

flip the pages
of *Sunset* magazine
                         with my right hand.
Rub the toothed edge
of the Smiths' house key
                         with my left.

She finally heads upstairs herself.

I know how
to deal
with Grand-maman.

You wait her out.

It may not be the nice way—
planning to shed virginity
in my neighbors' house—
but I know Brendan'll agree

it's nicer than doing it in the car.

You Know It's True

I never had a boyfriend
before there was   *B r e n d a n.*

It wasn't because I chased anyone.
I'm confident the reason   *i s*

because there was this perfect
person waiting for me.   *M y*

ideal. When we're together, we're
the only people in the   *w o r l d.*

At the Smiths'

Suddenly, weirdly
shy with one another
we sit on the floor
backs against the couch
huge blank screen in front of us
packet of condoms next to us.

"We could just watch TV," he says.

And I can't tell if he's serious.

"If that's what you want."
I try to make it sound flirty,

which works because
    he gently, gently
        touches that spot
            behind my earlobe
leans in
    and softly, softly
        kisses my lips.

Somewhere a clock ticks.

"Are you sure about this?"

"I love you."

"And I love you."

"Then yes."

Mouth again
brushes
lingers

longer
deeper

his shaking fingers
unbutton my shirt.

Mine
shake
too

a joyful shiver

when I

touch him.

No Guidebook

Her lips
sweet

tongue
sweeter still

skin
to skin

thrumming
joy

And no way to prepare

      touching
      her

      softest
      neat

      tucked up
      away

      jealous
      want
      washes

wait

Please, God

hold

held
meld

hers

mine

all one.

Prayer answered.

(BRENDAN)   (Vanessa)

SEx Maniac

I can't get enough   Now Brendan and
of Vanessa, her   I are connected at
skin, her hair   the hip as they say
her eyes   or someplace
her smell   a little
her hands   lower,
their touch.   or higher
I was in a bad place   (at the heart?)
before we made love.   and we complete
She lifted me   one another.
out. I'm fine,   A nation of two
nothing to   and I'm
worry about   thrilled his dark
nothing to see   mood's a thing
here, folks—   of the past.
move it along.   Because
Am I stupid   how can he
to hope   be sad if

LOVE HEALS EVERYTHING?

The Next Morning

Banana pancakes
with fat-free whipped cream
fill the Styrofoam container
wedged flat in my backpack

their warm smell
mingles with the crisp bite
of eucalyptus
from the tree I climb
outside Vanessa's
bedroom window.

Glass tapped,
curtain pushed aside,
window opened,
entry granted.

                    "It's not the fifteenth."
                    She's smiling.

"Today's just because," I whisper—
even though her house is huge and
her parents won't hear.

They never do.

A year ago for
our one-month anniversary
I brought her breakfast in bed.

I've been doing it
on the fifteenth of every month
ever since.

I put the pancakes
on her desk and
we settle
into her nest
of quilts and pillows
kissing
touching.

I want to beg,
When can we do it again?

I want to feel THAT.
Want to be with you.

I'm out of my head
and into someone else's.

I feel like a normal guy, so
maybe I'm NOT trans, right?

Right?

(Vanessa)

Things Look Different
feel different
to me.

Some have more meaning:

> Brendan waiting for me
> outside the locker room.

> Our fingers intertwining
> when we walk up the stairs.

> The sense that we're facing
> the day, the world together.

Others have less:

> Mr. Mixed-Message Mathews
> showing off the piece I just made,

> a plate of singing blues, screaming reds
> fired in low heat to retain the

> vibrant colors that pale
> next to the best parts of

Brendan and me together,
our souls.

I'm Bothering Julie

and today she's
the one trying to focus
on the clay in her hands,
centering it on the wheel.

I'm just playing
with a blob,
rolling it with
my dry fingers
making a sphere,
then squishing it.
Sphere
squish.

I want to tell her,
want to tell Tanya,
but not here.

Sphere
squish.

"What are you doing tonight?"
I ask.

        "Tanya and I have
        our Spanish project."

"Are you guys working
at your house?"

        A shrug. "I'm not sure."

"Let me know—
I'll stop by—bring you guys
a snack."

          "No thanks." She looks up
          at me. "We still have gingerbread
          from YESTERDAY."

Shit.

Yesterday, the Sunday
after Thanksgiving,
we were supposed to
make gingerbread houses,

yet another tradition with us.

I can't believe I forgot.

"Oh my God! I am so sorry!
Why didn't you call me?"

               She flips the table switch to Off.
               "We figured if you wanted to
               be there, you would be."

10 Hours Later

I stand in the doorway of Julie's room,
a box of powdered donuts
in one hand, a huge bottle of Dr Pepper
in the other.

I'm here to beg forgiveness . . .
and to tell them about
Thursday night.

It's not just that I want to blab
that Brendan and I did it,
best friends tell each other stuff,
right?

But Julie's the only one here,
sitting on her bed,
giving herself a pedicure.

Not a Spanish book in sight.
And she won't look at me.

Deep forest green
slicks off the brush
and onto her nails
deliberate, slow.

I put my peace offering
down on her desk.

"Where's Tanya?"

"She already left."

"Look, I am so sorry—"

Julie interrupts.
"Tanya and I like you
and we like Brendan,
but we don't like you together."

"What's that supposed to mean?"
My hands are fists.

"You're so different around him,
always agreeing with everything he says
like you don't have your own opinions
—and we never see you
when you're not with him."

"That's not true."
God, I can't believe her!
"I'm here right now, aren't I?"

"Because he's busy, right?"
Julie puts the lid on the polish,
clinks the bottle on her desk.
A bossy, decisive sound.

"No." A twinge at the lie.

"It's all Brendan this and Brendan that!
We used to think it was because
you'd just started going out
but it's been over a year!"

Adjusts cotton between her toes.
No smeared pedi here.

"You're worse than ever
and, no offense, we're sick of it!"

They talk behind my back?
What bitches!
My eyes narrow

at her green toes.

"That's a perfect color for you!
You're just jealous!"

I slam out
of her room.

Her mom looks up from her computer
when I rush through the family room
on my way out. But I don't bother
to say goodbye.

Julie doesn't come after me
doesn't even call my name.

Driving away,
tears
behind my eyes,
a tightness
in my throat.

I tell myself
over and over
I don't need Julie OR Tanya—

I have Brendan.

Busy Schedules
mean rare family dinners
but tonight the candles are lit
and the table is set.

And if I needed
to be reminded
of how lucky I am
that there's not more
together time for us

I'd look no farther
than the other end of the table
where Claude the Interloper
sits—ranting.

> ". . . and I told Twinkletoes that
> if he had issues with
> my conducting he should
> bring them to me, damn it!"

My mother, seated to his right,
makes a soothing sound.

Across from Mom,
Courtney plays with
the food on her plate.

Lining up short noodles,
oblivious to the Interloper's
crappy idea
of dinnertime conversation.

We've been treated
to this topic,
      this opinion
before.

A year ago, Simon Adderly,
spiffy new first violinist,
turned out to be a
"special friend" of Viktor Jensen,
the orchestra's executive director.

And now whenever Simon
has questions about anything—
say the tempo
for some piece of music,

the Interloper comes home and
explodes into tirades
about this "light in the loafers" guy.

(And people in the arts
are supposed to be more enlightened?
Another stereotype bites the dust.)

"There's no way he'd be
bringing it up at all
if he wasn't
Viktor's little boyfriend!"

The real problem
isn't that a lowly musician
expresses his thoughts about music to
the "great maestro."

It's that he's gay
when he does it.

Claude the Interloper, great
conductor of the philharmonic,
stabs his food with energy
that would make
a serial killer's mom proud.

"Who the hell
does that little fag
think he is?"

The f word is going too far.
Mom touches his hand,
nods toward Court.

"Sweetie, that's enough,"
she says.

Tamed
(by her new breasts?)
he shuts up.

It dawns on me that
if he knew about Willows
my mother's husband
might actually, secretly
approve of my vandalism.

I eat my salmon
and try not
to think about it.

Saturday's Tournament
My lucky day.
In the second match
I pinned the champ,
Bechert from Hanover Academy.

A way better wrestler
(great defense, killer offense—
seriously painful)
who made a dumb mistake.

I went on to finals
while he languished
in the consolation rounds.
I won second,
he took fourth,
and his eyes were daggers
when I got the medal.

Riding the yellow bus
back to school,
Vanessa curled against me,
feels like another lucky win
(maybe undeserved?).

Teammates drowse away
various injuries.
Singlets stiff
dried sweat
BO, stringy hair.

Vanessa touches
her second-place
medal for 103
to my second-place
medal for 152.

"Twins." She smiles.

There's a red lumpy mouse
of a bruise over my eye
which by tomorrow will be
swollen shut,
a monster face.

"You'd better hope not,
this thing's gonna be ugly,"
I say.

She laughs, low,
kisses me.

Even as I kiss her back,
a little tongue,
I wonder for a second
what it would be like
to have
that smooth cheek,
long hair.

But it doesn't mean anything.
Now that we're doing it
I'm better.

That word is quiet.

Flannigan, the thirty-five pounder,
pops his head over the seat.

> "Get a room, Casanova."

Vanessa flips him off
but she's laughing.

> "Drive you home?"
> she asks me.

"You know it," I say.

It takes a long time
to get to my house
from a meet
with a detour down to
Mono Cove—
its nickname earned
through the years,

a place to catch
the kissing disease.
Bluff hidden
private
tucked away
tiny beach
salt-air smell
in our noses
surf pounding
in our ears
aching bodies
come to comfort.
Questions slide back
                    the waves
                        at low tide.

I love the feeling
just afterward, too.
Nuzzling love
soft whispers
quiet jokes.

I wish more
than anything (almost)
we could go to sleep
and wake up
the next day
together.

Because Going Home Is Such a Ride

Rain-painted headlights
sweep past in the mist,
I stare at them
to avoid looking
at Willows
when we
go by.

I'm better
in my body
but guilty

in my brain
of taking
my freak

out on them.

And I know
I need to
do something
to soothe my mind,

my conscience.

Sunday Night at Andy's House

"You guys doin' it?"
His question out of nowhere.

My thumbs stab the controller.
"None of your business."

"Oh, Dude! That means
you're not," he says. Laughs.

The weird thing is that evasion
might have been the case.   Before.
I might've even implied
doing the deed.   Before.

It's different now.
This connection,
more than physical,
makes me careful.

I'm protecting her,
protecting us
protecting We.

I raise my eyebrows,
shrug, as if to say,
"What can I do, she won't put out?"

I'm very manly.

Online Before Bed

I feel even manlier
when I
figure out
a way to
make it up
to Willows.

To that girl.

I discover

the cost
of replacing a window
that size

equals

half my allowance
for the next
five months.

I'll send money
every week
till then.

And the final payment
will   wipe
            my   conscience   clean.

(Angel)

The Second-to-Last Present I Got

from the Sperm Donor
was a pair of boxing gloves
          the bite
five years ago, handed over
with a sarcasm attitude, I thought,
          of the belt
on Christmas Day
in the morning
          stings but
That night he caught me again
this time in heels and eye shadow,
          doesn't cut
Wilderness camp didn't work. So he
beat me one last time. "No kid of mine"
          like words–
and "Don't come back,"
the last present I got from anyone
          Freedom.

I Showed Up at Tía Rosa's

one-bedroom apartment
on Christmas night.

> *"Lo siento,"* Mama's sister
> crooned over and over-
> warm washcloth
> on my cuts. We
> sat on the edge of
> the tub.

My three little cousins
crowded into
the steamy bathroom
around us.

> *"Lo siento,* Angel."
> Eyes huge at me,
> my bruises.

She wanted to call the cops—
I didn't let her.
Lord knows I hate
the Sperm Donor
but I love Frankie more.
And no one needs to see
their father taken away
in cuffs.

I begged my aunt to just
let me stay with her.

She worked a lot.
Hotel maid in the morning,
cleaning other people's houses
later in the day.

I watched my cousins
so she could quit paying
the crabby lady across the hall
to look in on 'em

and it was all good

till Rosa's fiancé moved in.

Gonna Ignore Those Bad Manners

'Cause Baby Jesus's birthday
is still the Most Wonderful
Time of the Year.

After I buy Frankie's present
(funkadelic PacSun sweatshirt)
I do a little holiday shopping
for the kids at the center.
Yeah–I'm in school–
part-time job,
counting my pennies.
But, Girl, I know how
it feels to not get
one single present
at Christmas.
Like the world forgot
you because you
weren't what it
was expecting.
And I know

one lip gloss tube   if what you
isn't gonna erase   really wanted
years of getting a   was just a
toy fire engine   baby doll
action figure   Barbie
football   tutu
plastic gun   manicure set.

I'm all for what they call
gender-neutral toys.
Girls can like football
boys can play with dollhouses

and it doesn't mean a thing.

But when you know you're a girl and
you ONLY get boy toys
(and not the yummy boy toys you can
play with when you're older)
then Christmas is
the Most Suckiest Time of the Year.

So I fill
my dollar-store bag
with little presents:
shiny bangles
nail polish
scented body lotion

trial-sized Christmas cheer.

For myself, three dollars' worth
of symphony carols
plus a pair of red-sparkle tights.

Just call me Miss Santa!

Back at the Center

everyone's checking out
the artist-type hottie

standing on a ladder
painting letters on the
window we replaced weeks ago.

Willows has to pay for that–
insurance only covered the glass itself.

I pray again the asshole'll get caught–
a regular prayer on my list now.

I start to feel like that Grinch
and I hate it,

so I snap myself out by asking a regular,
Daniella, to help me wrap presents.

I'll leave some without cards
for extra just in case
but there's a set of hair clips
I know have to go to Liberty.
They have hummingbirds,
her totem I guess you'd say.

Daniella cops an attitude.

> "Why you give anything to
> THAT skank? She pumps!"

Some girls do.

Not safe
but hard sometimes
to wait for hormones
to kick in
and even with their help,
you usually wind up a cup size
smaller than your mama-
so if your mama
had no tits to speak of,
you won't either.
Not without surgery
or pumping.

Some girls
think pumping
is trashy-
judge those who go
to pumping parties,
strip down in apartments
or hotel rooms,
let someone with
no medical connection
inject that silicone
right into their
chests, hips, lips.

Dangerous, like I said.
Lopsided tits sometimes
aren't the worst of it-
silicone gets in your lymph nodes
or lungs and shit.

I hand the tape to Daniella. I usually try
not to preach–but sometimes . . .

"Girl? Don't you know
it's the season of kindness?

"Your tolerance would be the
best present for everyone.

"Including yourself."

She's huffy, but quiet.

Thinking, I hope.

Because Honestly
is it trashy
to want something so bad
you go for it
even if it might kill you?

My opinion?

It's judging that's trashy.

Bad enough the world looks at us
under a (distorted) microscope.

Like the good Lord says,
we don't need to
judge each other.

(BRENDAN)

O
Christmas Tree.
"Wake up! Up! Up! Up!"
Courtney jumping on my bed.
I open one eye (the only one I can).
"Go away, squirt." "Get up! We're getting
a tree!" Every year, even without Dad, Chase
Family Tradition. Four-hour
round-trip to kill a tree for Christ.
We wear flannel shirts, pose for the
holiday card: "Look! A family of lumberjacks
living in the wilds of Wisconsin" or
something. Mom fills a thermos:
hot chocolate. (It must get down to fifty
degrees two hours northeast of San Diego,
got to stave off hypothermia.) She's mad
about my eye. "It'll spoil
the Christmas card!" Claude claps
me on the shoulder. "It just shows the
world he's the man!" He's proud. Like he's
the one who got injured and still went on to
pin the kid from Lind High to the mat. Must be
hard to be a nerdy philharmonic
orchestra conductor when you have
the soul of a caveman. Still, I go along.
Flex my muscles, wield the saw, wipe my
brow, sniff my pits, smile for the camera, gulp
hot chocolate, burp without apology.
I AM THE MAN.
No   Doubt
About   It.

Home from the Ordeal

Claude the Interloper uncoils
white twinkle lights while
Mom puts cinnamon rolls
in the oven.

Court settles in
at the coffee table,
an explosion of markers,
Mom's stationery and envelopes
a mess around her.
She's writing Santa a letter.
                    "Looky, looky!"
                    So proud.
"Very good,"
I tell her, though it's
just her name over and over—
the only thing she knows how to spell.

                    "Can you help her?"
                    Mom calls from the kitchen.

"Sure—just a minute."
I grab a handful
of blue envelopes
to take up to my room.

I'll send
them to
Willows with
cash inside

and
some-
day
be
able
to
forget
about
that   night.

When I head back down
to take dictation
from a five-year-old

I'm feeling pretty good.

(Vanessa)

Early Christmas Present
from my mom.
We're in the kitchen.
I'm inhaling a plate
of apple slices,
she's keeping me company.

>   "Oh, I almost forgot!"
>   She grabs something
>   from her purse,

hands me
tickets to the *Nutcracker* matinee.

>   "I thought you could take Julie
>   or Tanya." She's smiling.

Guess she hasn't noticed
I don't really hang out with them
too much anymore.

I called Tanya again to apologize
but she just repeated what Julie said,
like a parrot:

>   "We like you and we like
>   Brendan, but we don't
>   like you together."

and that's bullshit.

I'm sorry if they're mad
but there's nothing I can do about it.
It'll blow over eventually. Until then . . .
"I'll take Brendan," I say.
As if he wants
to watch ballet
(like I want
to watch ballet?).

I get *that* look.
"What?"

Mom goes to the sink.

She rinses her paisley teacup,
part of a set I made for
her birthday,
then comes back
to sit with me.

       "I'm glad you and Brendan
       enjoy each other"—

I can tell she's being careful—

       "but it would be a mistake to
       exclude everyone else."

She does that serious-Mom
look-you-right-
in-the-eye thing.

"There's so much more
to life than having a boyfriend—
and you need your friends, too."

"Are you saying
I can't bring Brendan?"

"I'm just saying you
should think about
what's really important,
what has lasting value."

"I'm inviting Brendan."

She shakes her head, exasperated.

"Do what you want."

She gives up so easily.

"Perfect," I say.

I always win.

And Speaking of Perfection

I've discovered
it's not in friendship
it's not in good grades
it's not in a well-thrown pot
it's not in a flawlessly wrestled match.

Perfection is the warm feeling
in the deep of my stomach
when his eyes meet mine,

and the memory
of what we did last night
vibrates between us.

The way he touched my face
   kissed my eyelids
      stroked my hair
         caressed my hip
           murmured love.
The way our bodies melded
and there was no telling
where one ended
and the other began.

   Perfection is
   the two of us
   together.

No lecture can change that.

(Angel)

"Phewie, That Stinks!"
Denai opens the living room window,
lettin' out the smell of acrylic.

Gennifer's doing my fills.
Handy to have a roommate
in cosmetology school.
Haven't let her touch my hair yet
but nails are fair game.

> "So is Liberty allowed
> . to come back?"
> Gennifer asks.

"If she apologizes to
the other kids at the center, yeah,"
I tell her.

Gennifer sets a little fan
to blow on my right hand,
goes to work on my left.
> "That all she has to do?"

"It's a lot when you
think about it," I say.

Liberty got caught
stealing from Willows
and Lordy, I'm mad with her–
and sorry for her
at the same time.
It was a blue envelope
like the one showed up last week.
Twenty-five bucks, anonymous donater.

Feels good to know
there's beautiful people out there
balancing the ugly.

> I pointed that out to
> Jason and Daniella,
> 'cause, of all the kids,
> they were the most
> shook up by the broken window.

Mailman brought in the mail
and I put the envelope
on the side desk for Dr. Martina
but by the time she came in
it was gone   daddy   gone.

I asked around–Daniella
said she saw Liberty take it.

Dr. M took kids
into her office
one   by   one.

Told me later Liberty
broke down, cried, confessed

and now she has to apologize
to "the community"
if she wants to come back.

I don't know how Liberty
knew there was money inside
but I know what she wanted it for.

Hormones
cost money

they mean
the difference
between
coarse hair,
man-bodies
and
smooth skin,
girl-curves.

The girls I know
who take 'em illegally

can't count
on a steady supply
of this remedy
that reveals
their true
selves

and they live
with the fear
of running out.

Me, too, once upon a time.

Roger Was Man of the House

and he let us know it
soon as he moved in.

I'd been living on her
couch a couple months
doing what I could

but Tía Rosa was grateful
having another "adult" there
helping with bills, kids.

He worked under the table–
construction for a
septic tank company

and she didn't seem to care
he smelled bad, like sweat
and dirt and cigarette smoke

didn't care he was rude
never said please or thank you
like she made sure me and my cousins did

didn't care he said
I'd have to dress like a guy
if I wanted to live there.

> "It just makes him uncomfortable,
> *mijo*," she told me. She wouldn't
> call me *mija* anymore either.

So I did what any
self-respecting girl would do.
Carried my clothes in a bag,

changed when I left the house.
I didn't like it but all shoulda been fine.
                    Of course it wasn't.

The last straw came
when Rosa was at work.
Roger in the bathroom doorway

beefy arms folded, laughing
to watch me scrabble around looking for
the medicine I hid under the sink.

        "I flushed it all."

And, Girl,
I wanted to kill him.

Didn't know how
I was going to get money
for more or whether

Lupe, with her pills
and injectables from Tijuana,
was even around.

        "Didn't look like
        no aspirin to me."

Before I could stand
he was across the bathroom
grabbing me, pulling

my arm up
behind my back.
I thought I'd pass out.

"And if I ever find out
you touched your cousins,
I'll kill you, pervert."

He slammed me
against the tub
then left.

Fire blazed up my shoulder, neck,
but that wasn't
the worst feeling.

I leaned into the peeling wall,
wondered how long I had till the
hormones in my system would wear off–

and added
Roger to the list   of people I hate.

I left that night
when everyone
was sleeping

but first I emptied his wallet
(only time I took anything
didn't belong to me).

Oh—and I called the DMV
to narc on him
for his unregistered car.

Guess you could say
I sometimes have a problem
with lettin' things go.

(Vanessa)

Sunday Afternoon
We go to the ballet.
(I promise bowling afterward
to make up for his having
to do a chick thing.)

At Weiss Performing Arts Center
the red velvet curtain
sweeps open to a
Christmas scene.
Onstage, children
dance and fight.

We slouch,
bored for most of it
until the Sugar Plum Fairy
comes out.

Brendan, suddenly
NOT bored,
              leans
                    forward.

We're only
five rows away.
Is she that sexy?

Looooong legs
blond hair

nothing like
chestnut-brown me.
I'm not the jealous type
          (don't want to be anyway)
but he's practically drooling.

I want to yank off
that stupid costume
wrestle with her
see how long
she lasts on the mat.

The next hour
seems like five,
hard seat
tense neck.

When it's finally over
I drag Brendan from the theater.
He's glassy eyed;
I'm pissed.

"What'd you think?" I ask.

                He pauses, suddenly cautious.
                "Ballet's not my thing."

"What about the Sugar Plum Fairy?"
I hate how accusing it sounds.
Hate my shrill tone.
Never let them see you jealous.
Grand-maman's advice out the window.

"What do you mean?"

"You couldn't stop staring."

"I was watching the show."

"Don't give me that!"

"What are you so mad about?"

"You liked her!"

He freezes,
knowing exactly who
I'm talking about.
Then he smiles.

"Jealous?"

I'm mortified.

"She has nothing on you."

He kisses me
and I should feel reassured, right?

But it's a distant kiss
like his mind
and his lips
are disconnected.

Crisis Averted.
But peace not restored.
Trans after all?

A bow-curved mouth
with lipstick I could taste;
that Sugar Plum Fairy was hot.

I think about brushing thick
blond hair into a bun.

Moving spinning leaping,
body light, spirit free

no extra flesh
between *her* thighs.

I jiggle my foot.

Do I want to do her?
Or do I want to be her?

Drum my fingers.
Quiet my freaky brain.

Bowling

is safer, kind of.
Get   our   shoes,
step to lane six.
The ball has heft,
it's substantial,
a heavy thing.
Solid and you
can count
on it to
do what
it's supposed
to do. No whining
that it would rather be
a football or a hockey puck.
Fingers slick, I hurl it hard, my

s h o u l d e r   s t r e t c h e s   o u t.

This solid, this strong, this unchanging
ball goes wild into the next lane. And it
knocks down the white sentinels at the
end of another alley. The manager's mad
(like I had the skill to do that on purpose)
and other bowlers are looking at us. The
kind of attention I hate. We finish the rest
of the game under their glares, inspection.

Later, just before sleep, I replay the scene
and know I wasn't knocking down pins. I
was annihilating the Sugar Plum Fairy
who   danced   in   my   head.

Next Day, Shopping with Andy Sucks

but not because of him.

Mall's stuffy and
Christmas lines are
as long as the plot
of the movie
he's telling me about.

Still, I listen.
You listen to your friends.
Even if you don't tell them everything.

Christmas shopping means
Where the Wild Things Are,
book with Max doll for Court.
Astronomy book for Dad.
The ugliest tie I can find
for Claude the Interloper.
A leather journal and a
cool-looking fountain pen for Mom.
> Two presents for her
> since her birthday's on the
> twenty-eighth.

That leaves Vanessa.

I want to go home
take a nap
play Diablo.

"Dude, you should totally
get her something sexified!"

Slugging him would
require too much energy.
"You're talking about my
girlfriend, asswipe."

"I'm just sayin'. Look!"
He points.

MAKING HOLIDAYS BRIGHT SALE
Neon panties in Victoria's Secret window.

"Come on, Dude."
Starts walking over.

"I'm not going in there."

"Dude, you know
she'd love it."

"I'm not."

"Quit being a pussy!"

"I'm not, you idiot!"

"Afraid panties will bite?"

"What if someone sees?"

> "They'll be all over you!
> The ladies love a dude who buys
> his girlfriend something romantic."

What can I say?

"I'm not going to buy
her underwear in front of
you, perv!"

> "Whatever—Lindy Carmichael
> works in there."
> He heads over
> toward the store.
> I reluctantly follow.

"So?"

> "I wanna go say hi."

"Why?"

> "She's hot!
> What's your problem?"

My Problem

is back in a big way
since the day
of *The Nutcracker.*

(I would love the irony
of THAT if I could love
anything right now.)

For weeks
that word had been quiet
and I didn't mind
my body all that much.
Not totally at peace, but it was
serviceable, functioning.

And sex—

    itself feels great
even if the parts sometimes
seem a little wrong
and it floats through
my head more often
than it should
that I'd give anything
to experience it
the way she does

from the other side.

Still, it's my body
that gets to feel it
and that made
the rest . . . livable.

But that's not
enough anymore.

I have to get away
from Andy's questioning stare.

"Catch you later,"
I say.

          "You're a freak.
          You know that, right?"

"Yeah, I know."

He   falls
           back
        into
            step
        with
me.

Arrrrgggghhhhh.

We head to GameStop,
shop a little longer,
check out
new games.

"Let's go see Lindy."

"Gotta get home—"

"C'mon, Dude."

He drags me over.

Satin and Silk and Lace and Perfume

A kaleidoscope the second
we're through the doorway
into Girl World.

Andy goes off to find Lindy,
leaving me alone.

And piles of thongs and bikini briefs
are strewn on the table in front of
women and girls
who peck through panties
like magpies or crows.

They have every right
to be here, to be at home.

I don't.

It feels awkward, I knew it would.
And I'm furtive.
What if someone guesses?
Illogical, I know.

But is there any logic
to the fact that I'm once again
Jealous? With a capital *J*?
Girl World isn't my place
but I wish it were.

Any logic to the fact that
everything's softer, better
or that I know
I could belong here?
(With the right body parts, that is.)

An extremely helpful salesgirl
(not Lindy Carmichael, thank God)
presents her tall,
thin but muscular,
near-perfect self—
asks if I need assistance.

Heart thumping,
I clear my throat,

point

to a mannequin wearing
a satin padded push-up bra.
"I'd like that for my girlfriend."
My voice strange to me.

The Girl World envoy asks about size.

I have no idea what to say.

I shrug.

She laughs, asks, "Is she about
my size? Bigger, smaller?"

My stomach flips.
"Bigger than you," I say.

Tense shoulders, dry mouth,
I wait for it to be rung up.

I punch in my PIN.
Transaction complete
I can
breathe again.

At the door Andy
catches up with me.
        "Scored a date with Lindy!"
We high-five,
then he
grabs the bag

looks in to see the gift box.

            "Awesome, Dude. Maybe
            now you'll get some!"

Christmas Day

Claude the Interloper
plays Santa and
Court tears through her presents.
Loves mine best of all
hugging squeeze around my neck. Kisses.
                    "Brendy, you're the
                    best, read it to me?"
And I feel good
for a minute.

I open my gifts slowly.
A video game,
some books,
and, inside a thin blue envelope,
tickets to see a hockey game.

        "Boys' night out." Mom smiles.
        "Just us guys," Claude says.

I know the tickets weren't his idea.
Maybe Mom's looking at it as bonding
but you'd think having been my mother
for seventeen years she'd have a clue
that I don't like sports.

Not even the one I play
because it will look good
on my college apps.

      (It's not just me—
      lots of guys don't.)

Still, it's
the wrong gift on so many levels.

Throat tight, I thank them.
Then it's off to Vanessa's.

Holiday-Schedule Bus

is slow
and after I get off
I still have to
walk up the hill
past a little guardhouse
where the attendant
waves me into the
gated community.

At her house,
a lingering kiss
under the mistletoe.
I hand over her gift.
She smiles,
hands me one, too.
We open together.

World of Warcraft and a
masculine thick bracelet
for me.

Name-engraved
stainless steel water bottle
for her.

A minute of quiet.

"You know—so you don't
always take mine," I joke,

but the silence stretching
like a lake between us
tells me I screwed up.

I don't know what to
say to her
about anything.

Wrong gift on so many levels.

And I'm a knotted snake of
love and guilt.
If she's disappointed in this,
how much worse
if she could
read my mind?

After a minute
of quiet she kisses me,
says thank you,
and we pretend it's okay.

Sometimes you don't get what you want.

(Vanessa)

Could He Be Less Romantic?
I guess it could be worse:
a tool set
or a book about
war atrocities.

I'm not materialistic,
but a water bottle
with my name on it?

And it makes me feel stupid
for always drinking
from his—
like it annoys him
every time I do that

when I thought
the gesture was
our little connection,
a welcome way
around his idiotic
no-contact rule.

I have to wonder
if he loves me
as much
as I love him.

I drive him home.
No time for a detour.

"See you after dinner?"
(We have a plan: ditch the holly-
and-the-ivy stuff,
later head down to Mono Cove.)

                    "No. Family crap.
                    My mom says I have to
                    stay home."

It may be true
but she let him come over
after dinner last year.

He doesn't look me
in the eye.

"Really."
It's not a question.

                    "Really," he says.
                    The statement is firm.

"Pick you up tomorrow?"

                    "Maybe. I'll call."

"Is something wrong?"
I ask. Stomach curling.
Was I bitchier about
the present than I thought?

"No—I just have to go."
He leans over
kisses me so fast
I hardly feel it,
then gets out
and practically runs
up the path to his house.

Merry f'ing Christmas.

Back at My House

"Did I hear Brendan?"
Mom's voice drowsy from her nap.
We celebrate *le réveillon.*
The traditional French feast
starts after Mass on Christmas Eve
and keeps on all night—she's tired.
Or maybe her mother-in-law's
long visit is wearing on her
very   last   nerve.

"I just took him home."
Slam into my room
before anyone can get
a look at rejected me.

"Honey?" Tap tap tap.
"Are you okay?"
Mom calls through the door.

"Fine,"
I tell her.
But of course
I'm not and she knows it
in that radar way she has.

"What is wrong with Vanessa?"
Grand-maman
doesn't sound drowsy.

"Nothing." Mom's voice
snaps shut. They both go away.

Crying into My Pillow

is

      a

            cliché.

I hate being a loser

but

      hurt

            feelings

leak out and

make

      it

            wet

anyway.

At Bedtime

even after the bath
that usually mellows her out,
my little sister
bounces around her room
on a Candy Cane Christmas high.

Mom makes sure Court brushes
her teeth, then I take over.
Where the Wild Things Are
makes her a little wild.
I pick up another story.

Beauty and the Beast,
a cloth-covered book.
No dancing teacups here.
Inky, dark illustrations
loom every few pages.
Courtney snuggles her head
on my shoulder.
A Johnson's Baby Shampoo cuddle.

I read the long story
thick with big words.

Court quiets, listens until the picture
of the Beast transforming to prince,
his face an agonized half-man mask.

She sits up.

"Why does he hurt?"

"I guess it hurts to change,"
I tell her, turn the page.

She turns it back,
points to Beauty,
watching the Beast
from the corner,
fright distorting
her features.

"Does she hurt, too?"

"I think Beauty's just scared."

"I wouldn't be."

But I wonder.

The Next Day

Caterers show up early
set their trays and racks
in the kitchen for
Claude the Interloper's
annual holiday party

in honor of the
symphony's biggest donors.

It's all about gloss and glitter
and as much Christmas warmth
as can be squeezed out of
a credit card.

My stomach
is growling
from the smell
of garlic
and pastry
by the time
guests and
favored musicians
start arriving.

They cluster around
my mother, who laughs and
chats and sparkles perfection
in a deep blue dress.

I spend most of the time
in the playroom with Courtney
trying to avoid everyone

    and the inevitable question
    ("Where are you going to
    school next year, young man?")
    that comes up every single
    time I'm introduced
    or reintroduced
    to any of these people.

Eventually
Claude the Interloper
comes to drag us out.

        "I have a surprise for your
        mother," he says. Courtney
        holds his hand, skips along.
        She loves surprises.

I follow them to the
meticulously decorated
living room.

The sound of
"Happy Birthday to You"
in four-part harmony
accompanies the caterers' entrance
with a gigantic harp-shaped cake.

Courtney squeals,
the Interloper beams,
Mom's eyes glisten.
        I hang back.

"Now there's a gorgeous lady,"
one of the percussion guys
tells me, nodding in my mother's
direction.

Everyone else's attention
is now on the
standard celebratory dessert.

Mom's beautiful.
High cheekbones
long neck
graceful arms
curvy outline.

She blows out
the single candle;
her audience claps

and my confused heart hurts.

(Angel)

New Year's
When I was little
my mama let me believe
the clanging pots and pans
and fireworks were
in honor of me,
her Angel.
God's little gift–
no matter what.

By the time Frankie came along
I knew better and so
we'd stand on the
deck at the country club
watching the bursts
and I'd say, "Okay, Frankie,
this next one is in honor of you,"

when the s k y

```
E               E           D
        X       X       E
            P   P   D
E   X   P   LO  D   E   D
            P   D   D
        X       E       E
E               D           D
```

"Angel, do it again!"
Frankie would say.

Little brother thought
I could do anything.

A brain aneurysm
killed our beautiful mama
and after that it was
adiós, madre dulce,
goodbye, little brother.

Nothin' I could do.

New Year's sucked then.
But this year's gonna be different
not like when I was working—
or even last year when I was
playing nurse to Gennifer.

  Her parents actually
  helped pay for her
  gender-affirming surgery.
  Making her outsides
  match her insides was
  the only way
  she was gonna feel right

-and that's cool.

For me personally?
Even if I could afford it,
it's just not that important
to how I see myself.

My junk doesn't dictate who I am.

Frankie's Back from Cancún
where he and the Sperm Donor
always spend Christmas.

I'm waiting for him at Denny's
so I can give him his present.

Then it's back home before
he's noticed missing–
and it's off to party for me.

He's really late.
I check for messages
every thirty seconds
in case I missed something.

Color me relieved when finally
crisp khakis, polo shirt, woven belt,
Top-Siders
                slide into the booth.

I lean over to give him a hug.
Broad fifteen-year-old
shoulders drop
STIFF as his buzz cut.

"Happy New Year!" I tell him.
"I got you a Christmas present."
Hold out the box.

"Thanks." He takes it.
Doesn't look me in the eye.
Doesn't open it.

"Go ahead!
I want to see if it fits!"

He unwraps the box
not sayin' anything.
Pulls out the funky PacSun shirt.
Something flickers across his face
then,
          again,
                    "Thanks."

The waitress comes by.
I'm about to ask
for a couple more minutes,
when Frankie says,

          "I don't want anything.
          I have to get back."

There's that look again.
I tell her I'm gonna
hold off on ordering.

"Thanks for coming to see me.
I miss you," I say.
Try to take his hand.

He pulls away,
looks around at the same time,
and I pick up what he's laying down.

Screw the Rest of the World

Who cares
what it thinks
of me–
but my little brother
who thought I hung the moon
and made the stars explode
just for him

is embarrassed of me.

I've been through some shit,
you know?
Both living on the streets
and off.

I've been beaten
by my father
and by bullies
and most memorably
by a sadistic-pervert john
who put me in ICU for a week

and the pain and torture
of physical therapy
for a long time after.

But I have never hurt this bad.

And there's nothin' I can do.

Brendan's Sick on New Year's Eve

and can't come
to Girard family festivities.

The adults are tipsy.
I'm bored out of my head.

I wish we lived on the East Coast
so it'd be over already.
                    "Why not ask another friend?"
                    my mother said, when I told her

Brendan wasn't coming.
I acted like I didn't hear her.

Now Grand-maman's eyebrows tilt.
                "Where IS that young man?"

She's shuffling the cards for vingt-et-un.
Her hands are smooth, a wax doll's.

"He's sick." If what he said was true,
and I feel bad hoping that's the case.

But I've only seen him
twice since Christmas.

He's gone through moods before but
he used to let me in—said I made him feel better.

What if he just doesn't want to see me?
My father pours more champagne.

He gets to my glass, I shake my head.
I don't like it. Grand-maman disapproves.

My American tastes are all failings.
I wonder when she'll disown me.

"Your *grand-papa* came to see me on
my birthday with a temperature of 39."

Way to spread disease, I think.
But I know what she's telling me.

Brendan would be here
if seeing me was worth it to him.

I suffer through two card games,
then my mother proposes Bananagrams.

Crafty, because Grand-maman won't play—
only English words allowed.

We move to the coffee table.
Mom shakes up the bag, letter tiles click.

"Is everything okay?" she asks.
She's quiet so no one else hears.

"I think so, why?" My fingers flick
the smooth squares. Rearrange five letters.

I usually like this game—it's like Scrabble
only faster—but tonight I feel slow, and

I hate that feeling of knowing ahead of time
that I'm going to lose.

We both take more tiles, and she says,
"I haven't seen much of Brendan lately."

I get an *n*, "broke" is "broken"   *(broken up?)*
and my stomach clenches.

(BRENDAN)

I Pretend
I'm in the right body, *a n d*
my slicked-back hair
is a ponytail.
I'm grateful *n o w*
the gray-blue eyes
I inherited from Mom
came with a matching set
of high cheekbones, since *I 've*
come to appreciate that even they
could be male or female.
I like the illusion.
(What else have I *g o t*?)
For the moment,
this moment alone,
illusion's enough.
The thought that it
might not always be is *a n o t h e r*
more radical issue entirely.
I cross my legs
tuck myself under
love how I look when I'm alone.
The crowning touch,
under a plain T-shirt,
came from Victoria's *S e c r e t*.

A Forbidden Jewel

in a shimmering gift box,

it sat at the back of my closet
for over a week

and images of Bugs Bunny
ran through my head.

When he wore a coconut bra
it didn't make him female.

Padded green satin
won't make me a girl either,

but I wanted
to see myself.

Tonight Mom and
Claude the Interloper
are safely off with their
New Year's Eve–concert audience.

Courtney, worn out
from jumping
on the trampoline,
is safely off to sleep
after I read her four books.

I unwrapped
the package
containing this
symbol
emblem
bra

inside my chest
a furnace.
Excitement
battling
fear.

You know Pandora.   Her box?
Nothing on me.   And mine.

I fumbled,
caught up
straps too short
cups too high.

I knew I
looked stupid—
turned my back
on the mirror

until satiny material
slid through plastic clips
longer, longer
just right,

struggled to fasten the back clasp
shoved away a rogue memory
of helping Vanessa get dressed.

I pulled on a shirt
looked down,
saw a feminine
shape and
                I was home.

My soul
had found
a shell.

Relief from
the gray sadness
of what I'm not,
a rising flood.

I imagined moving
through the world
alive and at home
in this, my body.

Physical form
matching my spirit
matching me.

But Cinderella Perfection Can't Last

The grandfather clock bongs midnight
and snapshots of
freaked Vanessa
shocked Mother
raging Claude
scared Courtney
etch my brain.

Pretending gets hard
remembering that everyone,
straight or gay,
would be
creeped out by this.
Creeped out by me.

I peel off my shirt
shed the bra
like snakeskin

      ball it up
    and stuff it onto
    the top shelf of
      my closet.

It's repulsive.
I'm repulsive.

If anyone ever saw
the real me
they'd know that.

Because of Frankie
I tried to stay in the area
even after leaving Tía Rosa's.

Not too close though–
La Jolla doesn't roll out the red carpet
for the homeless,
but San Diego's near enough.

There was a whole bunch of girls.
Trans like me
with no place to stay.

We shared clothes,
food when we had it,
tips on safe places to sleep,
advice on which gas stations
would let you wash up in their
bathrooms

without giving you too much shit.

Watchin' out for each other
and ourselves
'cause no one else was.

Well, except for
Renée.

I'd been on my own for two weeks.
Hungry, tired.

She caught me Dumpster diving,
took me back to her place.

Let me clean up,
bought me Taco Bell,
told me how easy it was
to make enough to eat,

buy new clothes,

makeup,

hormones.

All I had to do was . . . you guessed it.

Oh—and give her a little cash
now and then

if I was gonna do it on her block.

Only Friend I Still Have
from that time is
my roommate Denai.

We don't talk
too much about
what it was like for us
three years ago.

But every once in a while
we'll be at a table in Starbucks
or at home on the couch
and our eyes will meet.

I see in hers what I
know is in mine—
incredible gratitude that
we're still here,

that we got the life
we've got now.
That so far,
we've escaped
the
ugly
the
fatal
statistic.

Praise be to God.

(BRENDAN)

Tonight the House Is Quiet.
That word is loud.

Back against headboard
laptop on knees,
I "research"
bathed in
the dim light of
of my computer.

It's hard to see me
in snatches of statistics,
old words, new phrases
gnaw at my skull.

"Gender dysphoria" churns my stomach
with its science-fiction sound

and what does it mean
that I love Vanessa
mind soul body?

"Gender identity"
and
"gender attraction"—
two different things.

I snap the screen closed.
Not being gay doesn't make me not trans.

No Hope in Hell of Normal

If someone asked,
would I have
enough humor
left in me to say,
"I think I'm a lesbian"?

Vanessa used
to say
I was
a funny guy.

I think she's right,

but it's easier to laugh
when you're not

terrified.

A Simple Solution

And for the next few days
I just fake a sore throat.
It's better that way.

Better to lean back
in the desk chair
playing Warcraft.

I've signed on
with the Horde.
Built my Blood Elf avatar.

No more "research."

My shame stays in the closet and
I've found a way
to escape from me.

Virtual me has long legs,
blue hair,
a killer body.
It's as close as I can get
to being a girl.

I'm Larissa.
I'm Larissa and
I kick ass and
I can lose myself
in the anonymous world
of online gaming.

I start to think
it's all I want to do,
that Larissa is all I want to be.

The last weekend of Christmas break
is the perfect time to laze at home
pretending to be sick,
not stirring.

It's just better this way.

Except that

                    I miss Vanessa.

Final Day of Winter Recess

I leave the house,
drop an envelope in the mail,
show up to practice
tell everyone I got better,

promise Vanessa
we'll hang.

But during conditioning
that word gets loud and
something twists in me.

I duck out of the gym
catch a bus for home
stand under the showerhead,

let guy stink
go
down
the
drain.

She has to be pissed
I didn't tell her goodbye.

I just don't know
what to say to her.

Of course I love you.
Sorry I'm distant.
No, I'm not mad
just don't feel well.

Not sorry we made love.

Can't go out tonight.
Family dinner.

And that will be it.
There's no explaining
some things.

Others just have a sucky explanation.

(Angel)

Gorgeous Sunday
and I'm singin' at church like
music brings me closer to God.

When I was little,
Mama always took us to Mass.
The Sperm Donor
wasn't big on worship,
so he stayed home.
Sometimes if Frankie fussed
she'd take him
into the cry room
at the back of the chapel,
leave me alone in the hard pew
with wintergreen Life Savers.

I spent my time looking
at the stained glass window
of the Three Kings,

wishing I could wear
their dresses,

the colors were
so gorgeous,
so rich.

Later on,
I really
started listening

and realized that
even if
I liked church,

with its soaring music
and beautiful art,

church didn't like people like me.

After Mama's funeral
we just stopped going and
I sure as hell didn't miss it

until . . .

Three Years Ago
after a sadistic-pervert john
landed me in the hospital

Social Services got in touch
with the Sperm Donor.

He wouldn't take me back.
(I wouldn't of gone with him anyways.)

Got a social worker named Pat
who placed me with my foster mom.

Praise be to Jesus.

Girl, Veronica was homely.
Fashion? Forget about it!

It didn't matter, though.
Her heart was beautiful

and big enough
to take in kids like me.

She cleaned me up
brought tea, protein shakes

while my jaw was
still wired shut.

Big Macs when it healed.

She read books out loud
when the headaches
were too bad for me
to keep my eyes open.

Told me how smart I was,
how beautiful.

How valuable
my life to God.

I lived with her almost two years,
kids came and went,
bouncing around in the system.

(And I know now
how blessed I truly was
after hearing stories
from the ones who didn't get
a Veronica in their life
soon enough.)

But I didn't have
anywhere to bounce
and she said me and her
were a good fit.

When I healed enough
to get around
she invited me to her church,
said it was up to me though.

So I waited
and then waited
some more.

> (Till I was bored out of my brain.
> And we were used to each other.
> And I was feeling bad 'cause
> I stayed out late one night.
> And didn't call
> 'cause it's hard
> to live with house rules
> when you been on your own.
> And she cried when I finally
> did get home 'cause she worried
> but she didn't tell Pat on me.
>
> Girl, did I feel guilty.)

Funny thing was,
when finally I did go with her?

Church was a serious party!

Singin', swaying, witnessing
to the loving power of God.

Christ Church Unified.
LGBTQ friendly.
They welcomed me
embraced me.

Now that's what I call Christian.

Sundays Like Today

when there's nothin' goin' on
it feels good to go
to church

but I don't feel
like I have to
or the Lord will get mad.

I'm a pretty strong spirit myself.
And me and God?
We're tight.

We don't need anyone
to translate
for either of us.

God doesn't make mistakes.
I'm here for whatever reason He/She has.
No need

to apologize
For who I am.
For what I am.

(Vanessa)

Today Was Just Another Crappy Day

in a long line of
other crappy days. I *d o n' t*
know what's wrong.

Brendan left without
saying goodbye.
We were supposed
to hang out after wrestling,
but that was something
he obviously didn't *w a n t.*

When I left the gym I saw
someone'd written "dyke" on my car.
I acted like I didn't care—and
Brendan's the only one
I'd complain about it *t o.*

They say I play for both teams
but there's not a lot of play
now anyway. We used to
get busy after meets—
endorphins would surge,
win or *l o s e.*

Today he just left, and I wish
to God he'd open up,
tell me for real
what's wrong with *h i m.*

In the Parking Lot

I text him:
Give me a call?

By the time I get home
there's still no reply.

Hellooooeeee?
Nothing.

After dinner
I call his cell,
leave a message.

"We need to talk."

Nada.

I'm mad
and worried
at the same time.
There should
be a name for this
                    Morried? Wad?
I dial again, hang up.
Should I call the house?

Anger and sadness
compete inside me.

It's a tie.

(BRENDAN)

On the Wall

After my shower I
go to put on pants
and I end up in bed,
eyes closed. Won't look
at the dresser   *m i r r o r.*

How do you deal when
what you see just   *d o e s n 't*
reflect your soul?

The hips, the tits don't exist
and what is there is a   *l i e.*

The Big Question

I've ignored two texts and a call.
When I hear the landline ring
I get off the bed, still ignoring
the bastard mirror,
open *Hamlet*, and sit at my desk.

Mom knocks on the door.
(I knew she would.)
Opens it a crack
and pokes her head in,

"Sweetie, it's Vanessa?"

(I knew it was.)
I shrug.
"Studying," I say.

Mom nods—
like she believes me.
"I'll tell her to call back?"

She sounds like she's asking
a question. She's not.

Until she does.
"Brendy, are you all right?"

Oh, so there's ANOTHER question, not
just to be or not to be. Hamlet, you asswipe, you had it all wrong.

Thank you, Mom. The obvious answer
is NO. I've got a boatload of essays to
write, studying to do, and also wrestling
to condition for. A history project to
work on. And then there's the
matter of a girlfriend I can't make
happy. Because I can't let her,
can't let anyone see I don't just
want to be with her, I want
to BE her, and how sick is
it that when we touch I wish
my skin were that soft, my
hands that small. That I had
the same little hollow between
belly and hip she does. What the
hell is wrong with me? It's all too
much and I know that all the Zoloft
Dr. Andrews prescribes for my sad, sorry
teenage depression might've been a help
for Hamlet (lamest emo dude of the ages),
but no amount of Zoloft or Prozac or even
booze or praying, for that matter, can ever
be able, will ever be able, to help me.
What's wrong with me can't be

F
I
X
E
D

I Can Tell

Mom's standing
outside the door
still waiting
for me to answer.

"Just tired," I say.

       "Okay."

Is that relief in her voice?

       "Let me know if you
       need anything."

I hear her move off down the hall.

Knowing what I need is different
than knowing what I don't.

I don't need
to let the world
see me

a curious shemale.

(Vanessa)

Driving to Brendan's
feels a little weird.

I didn't tell him
I'm coming over

not that I always do—

but this is deliberate
as if I'm mounting
a sneak

attack.

His mom
answers

> "Vanessa!!!"
> Like I'm her long-lost daughter.
> She opens the door wider to let me in.
>
> "It's good to see you!" she says
> before waving me up
> to Brendan's room
> with a graceful harp-player hand.

He's sitting
at his desk
back to the door

World of Warcraft
on the screen
in front of him.

No idea I'm behind him.

I watch him for a minute
his shoulders are slouchy,
his hair a little long.

I want to touch it,
trim it, take care of him.

"What's wrong?"

He jumps
at my voice
turns off the game
like it was porn
or something.

"When did you get here?"
He doesn't sound happy to see me.

"Just now.
What's wrong?"

I repeat.
He stares at me a minute.

I can't read his face
and I want to cry.

Not long ago
I wouldn't have had to
try to decipher anything.

He'd tell
me everything.

        "I started feeling sick again,"
        he finally says.

"And you couldn't text?
You couldn't call?"

I'm getting whiny
and I hate it
but his excuse is lame.

        "Look, I'm sorry.
        But I don't feel well."

"And there was
no way of
letting me know that?
I was worried!"

His mouth
hardens.
"It's not always
about you!"

He flops
onto his bed,
closes his eyes.

"I really feel sick. I'm sorry.
Can we argue about this later?"

He looks tired,
small somehow
and maybe he IS
just sick?

Guilty
          I
                    cave
                              kiss him
                                        leave.

On the Way Home

I'm rewarded
with a text

for dropping
the whole thing.

ILY

And it sucks that
Grand-maman was right again.

She has a cautionary saying (of course)

Foxes are all tail,
Women are all tongue.

I think it means

shut up
if you want a guy
to love you.

Dr. Do-Little's Office

Soothing beige
stucco walls
press in on me
at my mandatory
six-month check-in.

I missed school today
so Mom could roll her eyes
and drop me off
at Dr. Andrews's office,
where he asks
the same old questions.
                    (Suicidal thoughts?
                    Tendencies?)

Last night I had the princess dream
and maybe agitation seeps out
in my "no"
because he doesn't take it
for an answer.

NOW he wants me to talk
and I wish he'd just
give me the prescription
so I can go home and sleep.

School's fine.
Friends are fine.
Wrestling's fine.
Girlfriend's fine.
Fine.
Fine.
Fine.
But not.
And I can't help it
can't help myself.

I fail at
being a boyfriend,
being a guy
and I'll never be able
to live as anything else.

And somehow,
thinking these things,
         (in the presence
         of a trained professional
         who nods and smiles)
but knowing I will
never
ever
be able to tell anyone

pisses me off.

I'm Lonely Without Brendan

Too much time
to wonder and worry
about what's *e a t i n g*
him. There's no one to talk to
and nothing to look forward to
when he's not here.
I miss him at *l u n c h*
and on break I sit in my car
thinking about next year
when he'll be off to college
and I'll be here.
Left all *a l o n e.*

We're Practicing Takedowns

After fifty burpies
a hundred push-ups
countless squats

my ponytail
is wet and stringy
by the time we
partner up
for my favorite drill.

Thoughts of
Brendan
leak away in
my pouring sweat.

I shoot fast
grab Sheahan,

who, after two years
as my workout partner,
is so over any idea
that I'm a fragile girl.

I take him down.
We stand up
do it again
over and over.

I'm in the zone
and he's tired

but when I hear the stop whistle
I take him again
'cause I can.

He calls me a dick
then bumps my fist with his.
We share a tired smile.

At tournaments
there's always
some buzz
in my weight class
about whether
a win by me
is legitimate.
The only way to make sure
is if my opponent goes for it—
lets go of the thought I'm a girl.

After all this time,
it's an easy thing
for Sheahan (my friend?) to forget.

I just hope that's not
what's happened
with Brendan.

(Angel)

When I Have Time
I don't mind
doing dishes.
Like it, even.

The smell
of lavender detergent
from Trader Joe's
reminds me of my mama.
I'm standing at the sink
thinking of her, of Frankie,
when Denai floats in.

Lit up like that Christmas tree
we still need to take down.

"Sistah, you are glowing!"
I turn, get a good look.
"Is that my sweater?"

     "Mmmhmmm." She's dreamy.
     "I knew you wouldn't mind."

I hand her a towel
so she can dry,
go back to the spaghetti pot
I was scrubbing.

I've seen that look on her before–
envied it then, too.

It's that I-just-met-someone look.
And it doesn't
seem to happen
as often as it should
to me.

(Now, you could argue
that my standards
are higher than Denai's
and, Girl, you'd be right! Ewww,
some of the boys
she's put up with!)

But part of it's
what you could call
a difference in philosophy.

Nothin' to do with standards at all.

When (or if) to Disclose Birth Gender

Such a controversy.
The arguments go back
and forth. Ping-pong.

Denai passes really well—
doesn't see it as an issue.

> "I'm not gonna ask him
> what he was born with
> so there's no reason
> to talk about me."

And that works for her.

Some say it's a question of safety—
if he finds out later and freaks
she could wake up dead.

Others say choose smart,
suss it out, then tell. Or don't.

Chantal says it's my combat attitude
contributes to dateless Saturday nights.

Whatever. It gets me less boyfriends,
but I like to ask up front
if a potential date's a transphobic bigot.

Leave the disclosing to him.

I Pass Really Well
but there's one thing . . .

After I got out of the hospital
Veronica said her no-illegal-drugs policy
extended to hormones.

So I had to go see a shrink
for three months
in order to get the legal kind.

Dr. Hendricks gave me
a personality test.
I could tell the results weren't
what he expected.

> (Shrinks always think they're
> better at hiding their thoughts
> than they are. Either that or God
> has given me psychic abilities.
> 'Cause I can always tell.)

> "You have astonishingly
>   healthy self-esteem."
His "professional" opinion.

I shrugged.
I'm blessed to like me
the way I am

even if I like my body
on hormones better.

Not my fault the
world just isn't ready to
stop defining gender
the way it always has.

Nothin' to Be Ashamed Of

There's way worse things
to be than transgender,
let me tell you.

Rapists who rape
thieves who steal
racists who degrade

cowardly haters who
do shit like burn crosses or
throw rocks through windows.

   "Take it easy, Girl!"

Denai's laughing brings me back
into the kitchen.

   "You're gonna scrub a hole
   right through that pot!"

I look down at the bristles
of the brush in my hand.

They're flattened out.

Usually I know my own strength

but sometimes I don't.

(BRENDAN)

It Turns Out
moving through life
pissed
is better than
moving through life
sad and

wanting what I'll never have.

I keep my distance from Court,
who always wants a story. I

snap at Andy, who says,
             "Whatever, Dude."
Snap at Mom, who says,
             "Watch it, mister."
Snap at Claude, who says,
             "That was out of line."
Snap at Vanessa, who says
                 nothing.

And just before a meet on Saturday

I even
snap at Coach, who says,
             "That's my boy, go get 'em."

He cups a hand on my shoulder
before sending me onto the
mat to crush my opponent
from Jefferson High.

My wrestling's getting wilder,
technique less refined.
I'm on the verge
and my adversaries know it.

      "Take it easy, Brendan."

But there's no stopping me.
Even the fact that I've come to
really hate touching other guys—
swarming over and around their bodies—

takes a backseat to the unleashing
fury of this body,
this body that isn't mine.

My new maniac style
impresses Coach.
Bad luck.
Because now he thinks
he can depend on me.

(Vanessa)

Dateless, Friendless on a Friday Night
Thank God Grand-maman
isn't here to witness it.

She got on a plane
back to France yesterday
and my mother
looks relaxed for the first time
in weeks.

I'm flipping through the channels
trying to keep my
mind off Brendan,

who texted me
at six to say he
couldn't go out.

And I'm wrestling temptation
to drive over to his house.

Dad's out with clients
and Mom comes in with a
bowl of popcorn.

       "What are we watching?"
       she asks.

"Nothing," I say.

Flip, flip, flip.
She sits next to me.
Asks point-blank what's going on
and I'm pretty sure she
wants to know about Brendan.
I don't want to
talk about it—so
I tell her about
getting into a fight
with Julie and Tanya instead.

I don't tell her it was about him.

> "Friendships can be
> complicated sometimes,
> especially at your age,"
> she says, and
> strokes my hair,
> tucks it behind my ear.
> "But, honey—the truest ones are
> worth the ups and downs."

That's easy for her to say—
she's had the same best friend since
she was in elementary school.
They're like sisters.

Aunt Jennifer lives in Washington
but they still visit each other
and talk on the phone
and laugh at weird inside jokes
that no one else gets.

I'm sure the best-girlfriend thing
isn't Grand-maman's idea of paradise—
she's all about the guys,

but it's something
when you consider that my mom
has that AND she gets to have Dad, too.

"People, People, Settle Down"
Dean Johnston is trying to get
all 900 of us to shut up
for monthly assembly.

The gym is loud
but that word is quiet

and I woke up today
feeling almost okay.

Andy's sitting next to me
bragging about how far
he's gotten with Lindy
now that they're together.

"So you really like her, huh?"

He looks confused for a minute.

     "Of course!"

Damn, he's a big mouth.
I just can't picture talking about Vanessa,
or anyone I cared about,
that way.

We sit on hard benches
divided into classes
to listen to whatever
antidrug motivational speaker
the administration's
dragged in today.

Lillian Bruner
climbs up the bleachers,
steps over my legs,
and sits down between me and
her girlfriends.
She's the queen of Miller Prep,
star of the drama department,
popular, and surprisingly cool.

I glance over.
She and Elise Hart
are checking each other's teeth
making sure nothing's stuck.

A wave
of weirdness
washes   over me.

Dean Johnston is still
trying to get people
to shut up.

Lillian says something low,
her friends crack up,
and my tenuous okay feeling
sinks into something else.

I notice the way they talk and
laugh and touch one another
and I can't help it.

Everything makes me jealous.
The clothes they wear,
the way people treat them.
God, I'm even jealous
of their little vanities.
(You don't see guys
brushing their hair
between classes.)

I'm jealous of the way
they hug in clusters,
the way they always
seem to have something
to say to each other.

Contrast that
        (even accounting
        for occasional mean-girl
        bitcheries)

with

sweat-stained shoves,
murmurs of "Faggot," "Queerbait,"
and "In your face, asshole!"

I glance at Andy,
who seems to have finished
providing me with the
intimate details of his sex life,

try to imagine hugging him.

It's a good thing I don't want to,
he'd probably pound the crap out of me.

"Quiet, People!"
Dean Johnston
repeats into the mic
for the third time.

>   "We have a really special
>   presentation for you this morning,
>   brought to you by Plus Healthcare.

>   "Later today
>   your homeroom teachers
>   will pass out"—

Lil leans into me.
"Give them air!" she says,
even as Dean Johnston
continues his sentence—
>   "packets of information."

It's funny and I laugh,
one of her entourage

for a delicious
minute
in time.

In the Bleachers
Flannigan nudges me,
points across the gym.

"Check it out."

I look over to where
the seniors sit.
"What?" I ask him,
scanning the rows.

"Look who your boyfriend's
sitting next to."

Sheahan looks, too, shakes his head.
"Flannigan, you're such a shit-stirrer."

And it takes me a minute
to see what they're talking about

because Brendan's sitting
almost sideways,
his back to Andy.

I'm sick, he says
I'm depressed, he says
I'm just not in the mood, he says

and I've accepted his lame excuses

for the distance,
unreturned phone calls,
short temper with me.

And there he is
laughing it up
with Lillian Bruner,
looking anything
but sick
or depressed
or not in the mood.
"Shut up, Flannigan." I strike a bored tone,
                              outwardly calm in the
                              din of the gym.

Why doesn't he laugh
with me anymore?

What happened to our
Nation of Two?

Is it about to include
the state of Lilliandia?

There's no way he'd
cheat on me though.   Skin prickles.

Is there?

Thank God

ceramics is
right after assembly.

Julie is at the table closest to the door.
She nods at me when I walk past.
I nod back, too preoccupied
to think very hard about this subtle thawing.

I settle in at my table
to slam the hell
out of a block of clay.
Push and work
knead and fold.

> "Take it easy, Vanessa,"
> Mr. Mathews says
> when he walks by.
> "Be careful—I think you're
> working air bubbles into that."

I ignore him,
pound and push
knead and fold.

All tail
no tongue.

Oh, God.
What if Brendan
just doesn't love me anymore?

The Closer Finals Get
the nastier Coach gets
(a real motivator).

He's working
the team,
working me,
harder than
ever before.

(I'd like to see him
do a hundred push-ups
after rope climbing.)

> Training lasts
> three hours now
> and I hear his voice
> in my sleep,
> what little I get,
> because after practice,
> it's home to homework
> till one or two (and I'm down
> to a B in AP History),
> then gaming for an hour to relax
>
> and when I close my eyes
> I see a river stone
> sail through a window
> and that word gets loud.

My Insides Are Roiling

A concert tonight
means leaving practice early.

Coach didn't say anything
when I first told him
but that was two hours ago—
steam's had time to build,
and sure enough, he follows me
when I leave the wet heat
of the wrestling room.

Outside, the cool air
feels like an attack.

> "Remind me why you're leaving,
> when the rest of the team is
> in there working their asses off?"

> Chest out
> > aggressive stance
> > face pushed
> > toward mine.

I pull my head back
out of range
of his sour breath.

"I have to babysit my little sister."

He doesn't say anything
he just stares at me
like I'm diseased or something.
His eyes get squinty.

"Babysitting is for fags,"
he finally snarls, before
slamming back into the gym.

I stand there
a minute.
My legs
are still shaking
but not from the squats.

Mom and Claude the Interloper

leave as soon as I get home.
Courtney's still up
twirling around
in a purple dance outfit.

       "Brendy, Brendy, Brendy!"

I'm exhausted.
"Not now."

       "Now, now, now!"

"Later, squirt."

       "Brendy, Brendy, Brendy!"

She's hanging on me.
"I said later."

       "Come see, come see!"

It's all too much
she's too much and
my patience
snaps like a
balsa-wood glider.

"Leave me the hell alone!
I'm not your frigging jungle gym!"

Her face puckers.

But I keep yelling.

Because I've had it with everything.
Slow buses. Needy girlfriends.
Sadist coaches. Demanding teachers.

And little sisters who
dress like ballerinas
floating along
while I clump.

I'm unbelievably sick of
everybody and everything.

I shout it all out.
Her face goes from puckered
to screwed-tight eyes
to openmouthed wailing.

And I keep shouting.

She runs to her room.

I go into mine
throw my half-open backpack
against the wall,
     a paper avalanche,

try to ignore hiccupy sobs.

I flip on my Mac and
she's still sobbing.

My gut twists again.

I need to get a grip.

I've shouted down Courtney,
who adores me

and in spite
of the sick feeling that
I'm letting her
adore an impostor,

I know I need her love.

Icons come up
against wallpaper—
a screen shot
of my avatar.

I stare at it
until Larissa blends
with the rest
of my virtual world.

I get up and follow
intermittent sobs
like bread crumbs
to Courtney
in her room.

"I'm sorry, squirt."

        "You were mean!"

"I know and I'm sorry."
Stroke her hair
rub her back.

        Her crying, already
        slower, stops.
        "Be nice?"

"I'll be nice."
Smooth the back of her
purple dance outfit.
"I'll read to you."

She picks *Rapunzel*
and I want to groan
not just because I'm sick
of her favorite (I am)
but because it reminds me of
just how short my own hair is.

We settle in on her
comfy, cozy, pink bedspread
to read that tired tale
of the princess fair
with golden hair.

Still, she leans against me
and for a few minutes
my life forgets to suck.

I'm Finishing Homework

when Mom
and Claude the Interloper
come home
chatting and wired
like always
after a concert.

I hear them coming up the stairs
then Mom stops by my door
sticks her head in.
   "Courtney go down okay?"

   The Interloper continues
   on to their room.

"Fine," I say.

She steps through the door,
elegance in long black dress,
heels, and strand of pearls.

Completely at odds
with the mayhem
of my room.

My teenage boy's room.

Her nose wrinkles.
She looks around.
   "This is a disaster."

And I have to agree
even for me it's
pretty bad.

"I'll clean it tomorrow."

But she advances,
picking up empty water bottles,
and the closer she gets
the more uncomfortable I am
like she's going to find
something she shouldn't.
There's a plate from the kitchen
on my bed;
she picks it up.

      "Brendan . . ."

"I'll take care of it tomorrow!"
My shoulders tense,
practically touching
my ears.

      "Whoa! Don't you use
      that tone with me."

"I'm sorry! I said I'll take care of it."

Still sitting,
I lean over to scoop up
the mess from my backpack,
stack papers.
A little to my left,
notice that a
smallish piece of paper
with purple ink
sits on top.

That girl's number.

I put my elbow
over it
like I'm turning
to look
at Mom.

"I just
really need to
get back to work,"
I mutter,
tapping a pen
on my open
Econ book.

Why won't she leave?

Her eyebrows rise,
head tilts,
considering me for a minute.

      "Is everything okay?"
      she finally asks.

And I get the feeling
she thinks I'm hiding something.

Knows I'm hiding something.

It's almost 11 p.m.
We're going to have
a heart-to-heart now?

"Just fine," I say.

Arms full,
she stands there
looking at me a minute,
then stoops to kiss
the top of my head.

      "Let me know if
      you want to talk."

She finally leaves

and I move my elbow
off the
purple
sparkly
inked
paper

I had
all but forgotten.

I Think of THAT Night

Anxiety bubbles
      in my throat.

Is there *any* way
that anyone could've
seen me throw the rock?

Would I be recognized
if I showed up there?

But no one was around.
Right?

No one was around.

I'm going to have
to hope that's true.

Because

I need some help
figuring this out

and there's
nowhere else
to go.

Next Day's a Minimum Day

and I escape after early practice.

Home alone, I get ready to go.

Talk myself out of it.

Ready to go.

Not.

I feel like once that move's made
there's no turning back.

It will be weird
to group myself with them.

And weird to get help
from a place I vandalized.

What if someone recognizes me?
Or if they call my mom?

What's it like there?
What do I say?

      (Other than "Window?
      What window?")

Hi, my name is Brendan.
I think I'm trans, but I'm not really sure.

I'm not one of those people
who's always wanted to wear a dress.

Who's always known
he should have been born female.

As weird and confusing
as sex can be for me,

I still like it.

I have a hard time (pun intended)
wishing away something
that feels so good.

And probably,
since this is the case,
I really AM a freak.

I'm neither here
nor there.

Can't I just be
a girl with a dick?

I Get Off a Stop Early

and walk down the block
so the bus driver
can't tell where
I'm headed.

There's no way
anyone saw me
that night, still

my heart's pounding
like the hip-hop beat
thumping out of
the door when I
push it open.

        "Welcome. Can I help you?"

That girl, Angel, is sitting
behind a little table
and she doesn't seem
to recognize me at all.

I breathe, but don't know where to begin.

"I . . . I'm just curious
about your programs," I finally say.
God, I sound stupid.

She hands me a brochure
and an intake survey.

"Thanks." I start to turn away.

"You want a tour?"

I shrug okay.
But I'm holding my breath again.

Light purple paint
covers the walls
of the common room.
Sofas and chairs
a big-screen TV
some gaming controllers.

Right now
there's a guy in tight black jeans
doing DDR
while another guy,
in a thrift-store business jacket,
cheers him on.

Two kids about my age,
looking totally feminine
but a little . . . slutty,
lounge on one of the sofas.

"Girl, you so bad!"
one says, giggling.

He/she's painting
the other one's nails.
"Now hold still!"

I exhale,
breathe in
the smells of
nail polish,
hair spray,
and Axe.

The two on the sofa
wear thick makeup
eyes ringed with black liner.

A girl comes in,
taps Business Jacket
on the shoulder.

They both squeal
as if it's been ten years
since they've seen each other.

I don't think this is the place for me.

I fold up the papers
Angel handed me,
get ready to leave.
I just can't imagine
drawing attention   to myself

the way
they do.

Whatever else I am
I'm not
a flashy person.

And I wonder
if this is
how
I'd end up
looking.
Who
I'd end up
being.

Willows is
not my space
not my thing.

No help
for me
here.

There's bile in disappointment.

It's the Shy Kid from the Bus
the one reminded me of Frankie.

I look down
and this time his shoelaces are tied.

Frankie's never were.
Smart-ass would do it on purpose,
'cause he knew it drove me crazy.

When I saw him on New Year's
he wore Top-Siders
and I cried all the way home.

Group hasn't started and
everyone's just hangin' around.

I can tell it's a lot for this kid to take in.
Looks like he wants to run
so I tell the other intern, Lisa,
to take the front desk,
and I challenge him to Mario Kart.

I figured him for a gamer
and I'm right.

Kid hesitates, then,
       "I guess."

We wait for Tiffany and Eric
to finish their DDR
so we can have a turn
with the GameCube,
and we talk game talk.

Halo and Call of Duty,
Gears of War, Assassin's Creed,
Dead Space, BioShock.

And we talk platforms.
Xbox 360, PlayStation 3,
Wii. And PC games Warcraft,
Half-Life, Command & Conquer.

"*You're* a gamer?" he asks.
Emphasis on "You're."

I'm not the
stereotype PoPo,
girls can be gamers, too
but I get he has no
idea I'm trans.

"My little brother used to beat me—
then I spent about
four months laid up and
I got really good."
Quirky smile from him.
Almost smart-ass?

"Really good, huh?"

I know a challenge when I hear one.
"It's so on."

Eric finishes his dance
and steps aside.

I set up Mario Kart and
away we go.

The kid picks Yoshi
so I take Princess Peach

and I beat him two out of three.

We're done and
just kind of chatting
when I mention
coming to Willows
around his age,
looking for a healthy
trans community.

His eyes get wide,
then he nods,
glances at the other kids.

Shifty, like
he's not sure
about this place.

"I have to get home,"
he says.

I walk him to the door.
"Come back and see us anytime."

"Maybe," he says,
hand on the doorknob.

And I can tell he's never comin' back.
And I don't know if it's 'cause
he makes me think of Frankie
or if it's God tellin' me
this kid needs a friend.

We're not supposed to have private
contact with the kids at the center

and I do something I *wouldn't*

if I didn't know sure as shit
Brendan's never gonna be a client here.

"Okay then—
you still have my number?"

He looks surprised,
even more nervous,
and I realize the kid
didn't think I would
remember him.

"Tell you what."
I grab paper,
write down my info.

"Call me when the next
Mordock's Giant comes out.
I'll play you."

Of course I want to
help him if he needs it

but also, between school, work, interning
-being all-around productive Angel-

I forgot how much
I love gaming.

(BRENDAN)

Q Is for Question
(Holy crap!)
Angel is transgender!
She's feminine and beautiful
and easy to talk to.

And there's so much I want to ask—
like how do you know what's right?

What if you aren't always sure?
What if there are days when being a guy
only kind of tortures you?
And you just don't see yourself
as a supergirly girl?

(And how did you beat level five
in Machines at War?)

What does it mean that even if this body
doesn't feel like the right one,
high heels and dresses
aren't really for you either?

What if sometimes you feel like
you're pretending to be male but
you don't want to feel like
you're pretending to be female?

(Are you alone in this?)

And how can you keep
who you really are from
hurting your girlfriend?

Funny Timing That Boys' Night Out

falls on the day
I visit an LGBTQ center.

It starts with a two-hour drive
to Honda Center in Anaheim.
Just me and Claude the Interloper,

who wants to get sushi on the way

even though I try to convince him
that getting crappy food
at the arena
is part of the hockey experience.

> "Your coach won't be too happy
> if you don't make weight."

Like he knows anything about it.
I know to the ounce what I weigh.

> "Sashimi's pure protein, on
> the other hand," he says.

As if it's news to me.

> "Also, this will give us
> more guy time."

Exactly.
I study the menu like I care.
Order hot tea
so I'll have something to drink
while Claude the Interloper has sake.

"How's the girlfriend?"

"Fine."

"She seems nice."

"Yep."

"Which school is your first choice?"

"No idea."

"How's the new semester?"

"Fine, I guess."

It feels like an awkward date.
I'm not trying to be difficult—
I just have no idea what to say to him.
At least in the car we could listen to
the radio.
Claude falls quiet. Then—

"You still miss your dad."

I wasn't expecting this.
Tea burns my tongue.

>"To a certain extent that's normal.
>But at some point
>you have to man up.
>Accept it, and don't be a baby."

He sips his sake like he's said
nothing offensive.

>"I know you didn't choose me
>but I'm here for you, like a dad."

I don't need a father.
My blood bubbles low but no way
am I letting him see that.

I order four of the most
expensive rolls on the menu.

When we leave for the arena
I've tasted two. In silence.
And refused to let the waitress
wrap the rest to take home.

An asshole, wasteful move
that's rewarded by a
tightening in the jaw
of the Interloper.

(Vanessa)

Before Bed

I break down
and call Brendan
(*Get out of my head,*
Grand-maman)
ask about the hockey game and . . .

"I thought maybe we
could hang out tomorrow?"

     "It's Tuesday," he says.

He babysits while his parents
are at rehearsal.
"I could stop by."

I'm careful not to whine
that we've not hung out in a week.

     "I have to do a bunch of stuff."

It feels like a slap. I react—
"There's something
you're not
telling me."

Once the words are
out, I hold my breath.

     This is it.

For some reason
I check the clock
on my nightstand.
11:55. My heart beats,
sad, muffled.
11:56.

"I love you," he says.

I'm waiting for the "but."

"I'm just having a
crappy time right now."

So am I, I want to tell him.

"And I can't talk about it."

There doesn't seem
to be room
for more than
one person's problems
in our Nation of Two.

More silence . . .
Finally,
"I have to go."
His voice drops.
"I DO love you."

We hang up.
At least I didn't beg.

(BRENDAN)

Tuesday After Practice
I buy Mordock's Giant.

Courtney's in bed,
Mom and the Interloper are gone,
and Angel comes over. *S h e*
sounded happy when I called,
and through the guilt of
blowing off Vanessa, I'm glad.

Hanging with
Angel is great—it *d o e s n' t*
feel weird to sit in
the family room
playing games.

I'm so completely
comfortable I forget
she's not Andy and when
she takes an easy point
I give her a *p u s h.*
She laughs.

Even so—
I don't tell her
for real
what's up with *m e.*

We take a break
from Mordock, grab food,
talk about nothing some more.

She checks out *m y*
RPGs, pulls Renegade Road
from the shelf and
for a minute *g u i l t*
crashes the party.

        "You like this one?"

The cover shows a
bashed-in storefront window
and the burnt *r e m a i n s*
of a cop car.

"Nah," I tell her,
the back of my neck hot
remembering
that window   that night   that word.

I take it from her
stick it at the back
where it'll be *h i d d e n*
behind other games.

The rest of the night
is good though,
and when she leaves

I go up to my closet.

Heeding the Call
of the forbidden.

Wearing the bra feels
more natural now—

my body right
my soul at home.

And I let go of worry
for a few minutes.

The dread of upcoming
wrestling matches.

The nagging feeling
I won't get into any schools.

I relax as Larissa
in a way I can't as Brendan.
(Is that schizophrenic?)

I'm a little trans
but I think I can
keep it under control.

Hope licks away
at the rough spots.

Living That Part in Secret

And being Brendan-the-guy
in everyday life.

Mondays,
get set and go days.
Homework planning
for the week.
He's a studious guy.

Tuesdays,
Angel game days.
Parents out
Court in bed
play and talk and eat.
She brings up Willows.
Brendan-the-everyday-guy
changes the subject.

Wednesdays,
wrestling-match days
home or away
slick, sweaty,
furious, fast,
he wins more often now.

Thursdays,
family "together" days
means he's captive in the living room
while SpongeBob reruns loop.

Fridays,
Vanessa days
Mono Cove
salty sweet
tender taste.
Just a regular guy and his girl.

Saturdays,
chore days
mowing, weeding;
the Interloper
calls him "man."

Sundays,
Andy days
too-much-girlfriend-Lindy detail:
        "Her tit fills my palm perfectly."
And Brendan-the-everyday-guy grunts
the way he's supposed to.

He goes to school,
hangs with Vanessa,

sits down at the table
with his family,

reads bedtime stories
to his sister,

and dreams of the
freedom
that's his

at night

       alone.

(Angel)

Thank You, God, for Everything
is what I'm singing.
I seem to be all about
counting my blessings right now.

There's that San Diego sunshine
getting thicker by the day
now the rain is almost done.

Been having fun with my
new gaming bud
the last couple weeks.

Still hasn't told me
what made him
come to the center
        and I'm praying about that,
but it's peaceful knowing
all will be revealed
in Your time, Lord.

Willows's loss,
my gain
in a way.

Generous kid was shocked
I don't own a system.

(Not too weird when you figure
it's either games
or books for school.)

He texted me to stop by
and pick up
his old PS2 later.

I wouldn't feel right
borrowing it
if he was a client.

Thank you, God,
for Brendan!

I sing all the way to the center.

The air smells sweet and,

Girl, it's one of those days
just great to be alive.

Later, I even smile
when I look up from my desk
to see Jim from Adult Day Care.

"No beer today, Jim.
Let's get you back next door."

I leave Lisa in charge
and I take him back over.

Miss Prissy Pants isn't there
but Lordy, Lordy,
the specimen that comes to the door
is a FINE substitute.

Tall, handsome, cocoa-colored eyes–
models scrubs like he's in *GQ*
or something.

    "I am so sorry!" he says to me.
    Even agitated, his voice is honey.
    "They warned me about this!
    I don't know how he got by!"

I smile. "It happens to the best.
Jim here's a regular Houdini."
I'm feeling generous.

Handsome nurses do that to me.

Cocoa Eyes smiles back at me.

    "You work next door, right?"
    he asks.

"Yep." Now how'd he know that?
        "I saw you leaving
        yesterday."

That's how.

"Could you wait here a minute?"
He's got Jim by the elbow, gentle.

Lordy, do I want to but,
"I better get back."

Beautiful smile again.
"Teen center, right?"

All I can do is nod.

"Then you better hurry!
Who knows what could happen
if you leave for five minutes, right?"
He winks.
"See you later."

I turn, guide my
melty body to the door.

Hear him tellin' Jim they're gonna go
see what's shakin' in the rec room.

Funny, gentle, handsome,
I like it all. Except the conversation
we'll have to have.

(And that's if I'm lucky.)

Five O'clock, the Most Beautiful Hour

I'm putting my books in my bag
when Cocoa Eyes opens the door
pokes his GORGEOUS head in.

      "Glad I caught you!
      Just wanted to say thanks
      for bringing back
      my wayward charge."

I melt again, nod
even though my head
might fall off.

      "Can I buy you coffee?" he asks.

Disclose
      or not
disclose
         or not.

I take a breath.

"What do you think of trans people?"

It's a safe place to ask the question
there's other people in the next room.

Cocoa Eyes tilts his head
looks at me.
         "Why?"

Now or never.
"I am."

He looks again, closer.
Considering.

I'm dying.

"Do trans people
like coffee?"

"We're all different,"
I tell him.
Smile.
"I do, though."

We go to a shop around the corner.

Marcus is just as FINE inside
as he is outside.

We talk for three hours
and I'm late
to stop by Brendan's.

How a Girl Gets a Reputation
(as a stalker).

I'm glad Grand-maman has gone
back to the land of the
independent and oh-so-perfect women.

She'd sniff out what I'm up to
and I'd have no excuse.

I sit in my car down the road
from Brendan's house.

He's blown me off again
and I have to see.

Mom always says *Trust your gut.*
Something's going on.

I remember doing this last year with Julie
after she and her boyfriend split.

We hid down the street
from Ben Awami's house
and pretended to be private eyes.

It was funny then
girls gone wild
in a different way.

We talked and drank Starbucks
and waited to see if his new girlfriend
would show up.

She didn't.
Nothing happened except
his dad came out to get the paper.

He didn't see us
but we drove off fast,
laughing like crazy.

When you do something
you know is stupid
it's good to do it with a friend;
then they're stupid, too.

Doing this alone is pathetic.

Brendan's Mom and Stepdad Leave

and I scrunch down
hope they don't look my way.

God, I feel dumb.

I sit for a long time,
my skinny Frappuccino melts
and just as I'm about to take off
I see HER.

She's tall,
skinny jeans,
long brown hair,
pouty supermodel lips.

My heart whooshes down
I can't breathe
I can't even cry.

The door opens
and I can't tell who answers
but it has to be him.
She steps inside.

Who the hell is she? And
oh my God.

Is he seeing her?

There's only one way to find out.

(Angel)

Brendan Opens the Door
finger to his lips.
> "I just got Courtney
> off to bed," he says.

Takes me past the room
with the harp in it
and up the wide stairs.

> "I put the console in a bag
> for you," he tells me,
> still being quiet.

"You sure it's okay
for me to borrow it?
Your parents won't get mad?"
I whisper.

He makes a *pfftt* noise.

> "I bought it myself."
> He stops in front of his door.
> "Uh . . . I'm not very neat,"
> he says before opening it.

Eww, the boy speaks the truth.
He goes in and I see

bed's unmade
jeans on the floor
gaming controllers
tangled together.

He holds up Kingdom Hearts,
I nod, and he puts it in
a gym bag along with Call of Duty,
Devil May Cry 3.

We're heading back downstairs
when there's a knock on the door.

Through the side glass I see
there's a silver car in the driveway.
Brendan sees it, too,
stops, all twitchy.
          "It's my girlfriend." His eyes big.
          "Look, can you do me a favor?"

"Maybe . . ."
Not sure where he's headed.

          "Pretend you're the babysitter?"

"For real?"

          "I'm sorry–it's just–"

Now the doorbell rings.

"I don't want her to think
anything weird."

"There is nothin' weird," I say.

"I know, but she might think . . ."

More knocking.

He looks from the door to me—
sweatin', I can tell.

"Fine, I'm not gonna blow it."
I get in his face.
"But you might wanna
consider being honest
with people
you care about."

He doesn't answer.
Instead he

hands me the bag, abrupt-like.

Opens the door
on a girl.
Small, pretty
but not
what you'd call
friendly looking.

I step out.
Brendan's already waving
even though I'm only
about two feet away.

"Bye, Angel, thanks for everything."

(Vanessa)

Brendan Pulls Me Inside
shuts the door.

     "Hey, you," he says,
     sounding all normal.

He goes in for a kiss.
I'm a cactus but he
doesn't notice.

     "What's up?" he asks,
     like my stopping by out of the blue
     is normal these days.

"Not much," I say calmly.
Forget wrestling,
go into acting.
"What's up with you?"
     "Homework. Video games."
     We head
     into the family room and
     I can't stand it anymore.

"Who the hell was that?"
The words flame from my lips.
Forget the Oscar.

He freezes
steps back to look at me
shakes his head.

> "Are you REALLY jealous
> of Court's new babysitter?"

He flops onto the sofa like
he can't believe how small,
how petty I am.

I feel stupid
that there's an explanation
but wait—

"Well then,
why is she here
if you are, too?"
I have a seat.

> "Last night was her first night.
> She accidentally left her bag here
> and came to pick it up tonight."
> Exasperated, amused.

I turn my head away.
I know
I'm supposed
to accept this
to forgive him,
but adrenaline
is still rushing
and I can't—not right away.

When I finally look at him again
his face is serious.

"Do you really think
I'd be interested in anyone but you?"

His eyes are deep.
And damp?

"I love you
more than anything.

"You have to trust me."

I want to believe him.
I close my eyes.

Breathe
and breathe
and breathe
into the quiet.

I want to trust him.

I need to trust him.

I decide to trust him.

"I'm sorry," I say.

We   sit
staring   at
the   blank
TV   screen.
A   nation
of   two.
After   a
civil   war.

(BRENDAN)

My Heart

didn't beat for
ten minutes.

My   worlds   colliding.
Angel   Vanessa

Vandalizing   trans   boyfriend.

It took all I had

to act casual,
and then annoyed.

All I had

to turn
to Vanessa

after she apologized

to kiss
to cuddle.

And when she fell for
my Brendan-the-everyday-guy routine

I became the ugliest hypocrite
in the universe.

"Trust me," I told her.

But my lie is so much bigger
than anything
she could imagine.

Trust me not to cheat
    trust me to treat you well
        trust me to make love to you
            trust me to guard your reputation
afterward.

Just don't trust me
to be who I say I am.   I lie.

Guilt Is Beach Sand
on a second-degree burn

keeping you up
at night

no comfortable
way to rest.

> *Be honest*
> *with people*
> *you care about.*

Impossible,

right?

But maybe
there's a
guilt-lessening
trade-off?

Sort of
aloe vera
on a sunburn.

Not honesty
about everything

but there is something—
a position that will
allow for sleep.

1 a.m.: The Phone Rings
Fish it out of my purse
at the end of my bed.

Denai groans, covers her head
with her pillow—she has work at seven.

Caller ID says *Bren.*
Phone to ear
I stumble into the bathroom
so D can get back to sleep.

"Brendan? Everything okay?"
And he's off and talking so fast
my sleepy head can't hardly keep up.

> "... can't stop thinking about
> what you said about honesty
> and I have to tell you something
> but first I want you to know I'm
> already making up for it by
> sending money."

"Huh?"

> "Every week I send
> money to Willows."

And now I'm wide awake.
"Twenty-five bucks cash?
Blue envelope?"

        "Yeah."

He takes a breath.
I hear it.

        "And I promise I'll keep sending
        it until the window's paid for."

I'm all the way alert
but might as well be asleep,
can't think of one word to say.

        "Angel?"

Find my voice.
"You the one broke it?"

He starts talking fast again.

        "I'm sorry and
        I'm making it up
        because I really am sorry—
        I feel so bad."

"Why?"

        "Because I broke the window!"

"No, I mean why'd you break it?"

And now he's quiet
like he's the one can't

think of a thing to say.

"I don't know."

It's an effort, keepin' my voice low
so I don't wake up everyone
in the apartment.

"You mean to tell me
you threw a rock through a window,
freaked a lot of people out, making
'em think it was some kinda
asshole hate crime and
You Don't Know Why?"

"No."

At least he sounds miserable.

"But I'm paying for it
and if there was anything more
I could do, I would."

Which gets me to thinking.

He could come in and apologize
to the community like Liberty had to-

let everyone see the monster
under the bed was just some
punk-ass kid . . .

Only one problem with that.

Dr. Martina might not appreciate me
bein' friends with Brendan.

I been tellin' myself it's okay–
technically he's not a client

but he was a potential one
when he stopped by.

It's a lot to explain.

        "Angel? You still there?"

"I got a lot to think about, Brendan.
I gotta go."

He's quiet.

        "I understand."

I know I'm the first one
to hang up.

"No Idea What to Do,"

I say to Marcus.

We're drinkin' coffee
at his favorite place
and I'm tellin' him about Brendan,
the broken window, his sending money,
and how I'm not sure I can tell
Dr. Martina what happened
without explaining how I met him.

The Bean Scene has kick-ass mochas
and beaded curtains and jazz.

My favorite thing about it
is that Marcus is comfortable taking me

to places he likes to go.
Means he's not ashamed.

    "But he doesn't seem
    like a hater?"
       Marcus asks.

I swallow whipped cream.
"Nuh-uh," I tell him. "Even though
he practically threw me out
when his girlfriend came over."

    "Maybe he has a crush on you—
    didn't want her to find out,"
    he teases.

That makes me smile.
Marcus here's thinking
I'm so crush worthy and all.

"Nah, nothin' like that.
I know there's something
goin' on with him,
just don't know exactly . . ."

"You're so worried about him,
you can't stop thinking about it."
Marcus's cocoa eyes crinkle; he
leans forward–
kisses me. "I like that about you."

He leans back again
and I just can't
stop smiling
even though
that's not what
I was thinking at all.

One of my favorite things
is hearing what Marcus likes about me–
and tellin' him what I like about him.

I decide to focus
on that for now . . . Brendan later.

Angel Was So Pissed Last Night
she practically hung up on me.

I don't know what I was expecting.

I spent the day
kicking myself.

Was I expecting some
weird kind of
absolution?

> *No problem, Brendan.*
> *Thank you for confessing.*
> *You're a vandalizing thug*
> *but at least you're an honest one*
> *and I'm thrilled to be your friend.*

My heart's
a dried-up walnut

that only opens
at night

when I'm Larissa.

Hazardous

An unlocked door should never be.

Even with parents at rehearsal.

The door should be locked.

Even with Courtney asleep.

The door should be locked.

When it's time to be myself.

The door should be locked.

It's not about girly clothes.

The door should be locked.

It's about having this silhouette.

The door should be locked.

It's how I let go of worry.

The door should be locked.

It's how I forget about trouble.

The door should be locked.

It's how I like to do homework.

The door should be locked.

I concentrate better.

The door should be locked.

Words flow amazingly well.

The door should be locked.

Until they stop.

"Dude." Andy bursts in.

The door should be locked.

"What the Fu—"
He can't even finish
the word.

He's gaping
at
       me

      sitting at my desk
      in a green satin padded bra.

      No excuse.

      Nothing to say.

      This *is* what it looks like.

His expression

would be funny

if it didn't mean

the end of my life.

            He bolts.

Will He Tell?

We've been friends
since seventh grade.

He wouldn't
ruin my life.

      He won't tell.

But there's Lindy,

who squeals when she comes.
He tells me

intimate details
about his *girlfriend*.

      Of course he'll tell.

Awake All Night
I consider ditching
in the morning
but there's AP testing.

Throat dry
I go to school.

Andy and I don't have any
classes together.

Keep
away   from   each other
in the halls.

After fourth period
I see him with Flannigan.

They're looking at me
and when I hear them laugh
I know it's out.

My blood
pools
around my ankles.

I knew he'd tell.

And after school
I know my life is over.

Brendan Chase Is a Fag

Thick, black Sharpie screams
across blue locker room tile.
The hair on
my neck, my wrists, stands up.
I glance around the room,
metal doors clanking open
slamming shut.

      "What are you looking at?"
      Gil snarls.

"Nothing." Duck my head
focus on opening my lock.

A voice comes out of
a bathroom stall.

      "I'm changing in here, so
      the fag doesn't get a free show."

Laughter.
Then one   by   one
my teammates go into the stalls.

Rudy shoves me from behind
on his way past.

Stomach squeezes
ears pound
fingers fumble
with a knot.
I give up
yank my wrestling shoe on
without even untying it
grab my bag
push open the gym door.

Bad idea to
be in the locker room
when Rudy and Gil come out.

Rudy gets to me on the mat anyway.
Reaches into his bag of illegal tricks
to make wrestling really hurt.
Coach looks away.

And as I'm getting crunched into the mat,
and to be honest, half hoping
to get injured so I don't have
to wrestle at finals next week,
it hits me hard as Rudy's fists
that I DON'T have to.

My six-term commitment was up last year.
I'm quitting.

No Idea What I'm Going to Say

I don't bother
going into the locker room.
I wait for everyone to leave.

Vanessa doesn't look my way
before she heads out.

My guts are
on fire
but it will
all be over soon.

Door to the office is open.
"Coach?"

Voice wavers.
I'm ready to run
if I have to.

He looks up from his desk.

Brave Larissa steps in.

"I quit."

Even Predictable Explosions Are Scary

"Letting down the team."
"Not living up to commitment."
The steam coming out
of the volcano.

I stand my ground
but my toes twitch
ready to take off.

Behind Coach's eyes heat builds
until hot lava oozes words like "asshole,"
and phrases like "shit-for-brains"
but before they
cover me
I realize
I don't have to listen;
I'm not on his team.

I back up.
He really looks
a little crazy.

I walk away
fast with the sound of
"Yeah, walk away from me,
you little queer" echoing in my ears.

The halls are empty.

I know
tomorrow
they'll be
filled with

staring eyes
flapping tongues
pointing fingers.

Still, my pounding heart
slows, quiets.

I've always hated Coach,
I've always hated wrestling,
and if a school doesn't want me
because it finds out I quit before
the end of the season,

then
I hate that school, too.

Before Econ the Next Day

Lillian Bruner is
talking to Vincent Lindow,
her male counterpart
in the drama department.
She sees me, gets up.

      "Here, take my seat!"
She smiles.
      "I was leaving anyway."

And just before she turns
I see her
give him a wink.

He leans toward me
like we share a secret.

      "God, she's obvious!"
      he says.

I feel stupid.
"About what?"

      "Little Miss Matchmaker."

Huh?

      "She's always trying
      to set me up with people."

"But I have a girlfriend,"
I say, and it sounds stupid

especially since

very soon—
once Vanessa hears—

I might not.

     "I know, I know." He waves a hand.

I notice he wears three watches.

     "Lil's obviously decided
     you're my type though."

(Vanessa)

Flannigan Stops Me
on my way to conditioning.

"I'm sorry," he says.

"For what?"

"Your boyfriend's a fag—
he quit wrestling."

"Shut up, Flannigan."
He's always saying stupid things.

"If I'm lying, I'm dying!
And Andy says he
caught him in a bra!"

I stop walking.
A hot white flash
curls my heart.
I don't know what happened
between them but
that's a shitty thing to say.

Julie and Tanya aren't my friends anymore,
but at least they don't make up lies about me.

"You believe that?" I ask.

"Well—there IS something about him."

"Shut up," I say.
"Trust me, he's all man."

   "Maybe you're just a cover."

"Screw you, Flannigan!"

I'm so pissed I want to kill Andy,
who knows Brendan gets depressed
and spreads devastating lies anyway.
What a dick!

I'm sick for Brendan,
I need to go find him—

ditch wrestling
for the first time ever.

I'm headed out the door
when it hits me

that he quit wrestling
but didn't bother to tell me.

He's dumping me for sure.

(BRENDAN)

Vanessa's Car Idles Near the Bus Stop

"Drive you home?"

I nod.

"We need to talk."

A stone to my
solar plexus.
But she's right.

There's no way
she hasn't heard.

And there's no way
I can lie my way out.

I'm going to have to say it
and it's going to be real.

The buzz in my head
makes me
weak-kneed
stepping into her car.

We drive to Mono Cove in silence. I look out the window, jaw wired shut. I smell her perfume. We park and she turns on me, sharp. Says, "You're breaking up with me. Aren't you?" And it crosses my mind that she'll be breaking up with me once I tell her—but don't I owe her this explanation? Whatever it does? I open my mouth and

"I love you" comes first, then words dislodge from back teeth and tongue, pick up speed, tumble over. For a minute it's like it used to be and I'm telling her every- thing. My heart is pounding and I'm talking really fast, then I'm repeating myself because I don't want to stop talking, because I don't want to hear what she's going to say, but finally there are no more words and there are tears in my eyes and I can't look at her but I'm holding her hand; she hasn't let go but she also says nothing after I tell her I'm T.

(Vanessa)

You Know That Feeling of Falling

you sometimes get
when you're asleep?
Your whole body limp, heavy,
and you're tumbling off
a cliff and there's a thud
that makes you open your eyes?

Hearing your boyfriend
tell you he wants to be a girl
is the same sensation,
with no thud at the bottom
to wake you up.

There's Always a Choice?

I had a choice and
I chose Brendan.
Chose to ditch
my friends.

You choose to get up
in the morning
or choose to lie in bed.
You choose what to wear
and how to present yourself.

I can choose how
to respond to him
but I can't choose
how I feel about
what he chooses
to share with me.

So I choose to
take him home
but I choose not
to kiss him good night.

I Drive Home Numb

and stay that way
until I'm setting my alarm

and I realize tomorrow's
the fifteenth.

Then I'm madder than I've ever been.

Was he only pretending
to love me?

Was breakfast
in bed a lie?

Was sex with me
just a sick experiment?

And besides mad, I feel
used
helpless
weak.

I'm not used to feeling like a loser

and even when I've lost a match
I've always had comfort

knowing chances were
I'd prevail next time.

But how do you win
against something

like this?

If he knocks
on my window
tomorrow morning

I'm pushing him
out of the tree.

(BRENDAN)

All Vanessa Said
when I came clean was
"I see," and I wanted

to beg her for more words
but I was scared they'd hurt.

She drove me home
without saying anything else.

"See you tomorrow?" She nodded.
But that could mean anything.

And just the thought
of tomorrow, another day
of this so-called life,
exhausts me.

I go to bed tired of confusion
tired of being so alone.
No Vanessa, no Angel, no Andy.

Now I'm really alone
and I'll be this way for
the rest of my life.

No one will ever want to be
with the person who lives
in this body . . .

Not Me

With that insidious sensation
I'm in the wrong skin
slicing through my spirit,

though   *s o m e t i m e s*
it's muffled—
whispers almost heard

in that dark and murky season
when the last light is   *d y i n g*.

Who could love this soul?
Anyone normal or
right-thinking   *wouldn't*.

Vanessa used to tell
me to stop being so down.
Whatever will be will   *b e*.

Easy enough for her.
No doubt about it,
she's got her gender straight.
I don't and that's   *b a d*.

(Angel)

Surprise! Happy Birthday!!!!
For once in my life I am speechless.
Can't think of a thing to say.

Denai's holding a birthday cake,
Marcus has a wrapped box,
there's more presents
on the kitchen table.

Gennifer says,

> "Girl, you better shut your mouth
> if you don't want flies in there!"

I can't help it
or the tears that sprout,
stream, and don't want to stop.

Of all God's blessings
these friends are
the most important to me.

Marcus comes forward, kisses me.

> "Baby, it's okay."

And I smile even though I know
my mascara's running.

Three Years Ago Today

Cake, champagne, roses, chocolate
were the farthest things from my mind,
I tell you.

It didn't matter
it was my birthday.

I was workin' it hard
on the boulevard

tired and dirty.

A Chevy pulled up
baseball cap,
sunglasses,
Western button-down shirt.

"You wanna party?"
He wasn't my first trick
far from it in fact
and I ignored the tingling
at the roots of my hair.

(My advice? Girl, don't ever
let things get so bad you ignore
tingling at the roots of your hair
unless you wanna find out how
much worse they can get.)

Driving inland
nerves really
kicked in.

Baseball Cap
finally stopped the car
at a deserted business park.

Beer
belly
belt
buckle.
Throat too dry
to work
up the spit
I needed.

Still he got
what he was there for
and afterward
grabbed my crotch.
"I knew it!"
Slammed my
head against the dashboard
so hard my world

```
E                 E              D
      X           X        E
            P     P    D
E     X     P     LO   D    E    D
            P     D    D
      X           E         E
E                 D              D
```

came   back   together

in   pieces

dragged   out

        pavement

boots

blood

black.

When I woke up
I'd been 17 for 6 days.

Veronica Says

everything happens
for a reason.

Ever notice how
when something's a cliché
it's 'cause it's true?

Her only brother
died of AIDS
and her husband ditched her
'cause she never could have kids.

Sad, but if all those things
hadn't happened
in her life
she might not of
been there for a kid like me.

She was more than
just a foster mother
who cleaned me up
got me back into school
made me quit smoking (everything)
helped me check out Willows.

She even tried to get me visits
with Frankie–
till that asshole judge ruled
I was unfit company
for a thirteen-year-old.

In return I gave her
fashion advice (she never took it),
mowed the lawn without her asking,
rubbed her feet.

I was that grateful.

I worried 'cause I knew
I could never pay her back.

"Don't worry," she'd say.
"I know you'll pay it forward."

I hate
The Sperm Donor
The Asshole Judge
The baseball-cap-wearing pervert

but I'm grateful, too.

Why?
Veronica.
Willows.
The life I got now
and the chance to pay it forward.

Next time Veronica checks in on me
I'm gonna tell her about Brendan.

He's messed up
but I'm gonna find a way
to help him.

(Vanessa)

In the Morning
I'm putting on waterproof mascara
before wrestling practice and
the eyes looking back
at me are tiny.

Sheahan notices,
takes advantage of
my slowness
in the takedowns.

Brendan doesn't come to wrestling
and no one says anything to me
about him.

At Breakfast

I tell Mom
I quit wrestling.

> "I never could go see you
> after that first match.
> It just looked so awful."
> She shakes her head, like the
> memory will fall out.

> "I was afraid I'd scream terrible
> things at your opponents."

I'm a little surprised
she's so relieved—

Is that *really* the reason
she was the only parent
who never came to meets?

Detached,
I mull it over.
Dismiss,
it doesn't matter.

Claude the Interloper
pats her arm
like she's an invalid,

then invites me to get donuts
now that I'm not training.

Just great.

I know he's secretly thinking
I'm a weakling for quitting

days before finals.

Brendan and I
must be broken up
even though neither
of us has said so.
                    And how could we
                    when we don't talk?

He takes the bus,
I don't offer him a ride.
There's an empty space
where anger was
and in its place
                    my heart is breaking.

This morning I started to wonder
if it was all an elaborate lie
to trick me into dumping him
because he was too chicken
to end it himself.

And then I saw him
drooping down
the hall
and knew
there's something
really wrong.

I wish I had someone
I could talk to about it.

I Have a Question

                    things better than
     boy   those
     liked   meant for
     always   girls: football
     I have   to hopscotch
                                 blue to pink.
                                 I didn't even
                                 start dressing
                                 like a girl
                                 until people
                                 started
                                 saying I
                             was a dyke
                            for wrestling.
                            Now Brendan
                            says he's a
                    girl inside
                    and I
                    love
               Brendan.
                What
               does
               that
               make

               Me?

The Night Before Wrestling Finals

I turn out my bedside lamp
and when I close my eyes
an Erin Bledsoe memory
flashes behind them.

She lived
next door to me
until third grade.

Erin had bunk beds
and on sleepovers
we liked to be
in the top one together.

After popcorn
and a *Princess* DVD
her mother would kiss
us both on the forehead.

And turn out the lights.

It started
just before Christmas.
December break.
Stormy night
howling wind
thudding rain
prevented sleep.

Doctor, nurse,
boyfriend, girlfriend,
soap opera.
The games
built slowly.

Exploring
our bodies
ourselves
each other.

Hello Kitty
days-of-the-week
jammies
panties
discarded.

Touching
never felt wrong
at the time
but daylight
always left me   embarrassed.

We fought
sometimes
over who had
to be the boy

and I search my
mind for any
memory

that I ever
wanted to be
anything but the girl

or that I wanted Erin
to be anything
but the boy.

I can't find it.

There Are Phases

of the moon that
I learned in Science.

Waxing crescent
first quarter
waxing gibbous
full
waning gibbous
third quarter
waning crescent
new.

And, easy to remember,

phases of the seasons.
Spring
summer
winter
fall.

There are phases of life.
When you're a baby
child
teenager
adult.

And these
are all passing;
nothing stays the same.

I'm flopping, turning
in bed. Hot pillow,
no sleep.

Maybe Brendan's thing
is just a phase?

A strange phase. Like me and Erin.

Hard to understand

but maybe he just thinks
he wants to be a girl for now

and in a year
we won't even remember
this phase.

Kind of like
you don't remember
thudding December rain
in the soft touch of spring.

(Angel)

Nerves at the Sight of a Sweet Bungalow
set off from the street.
Sunflower lights
line the walk.

Lord, I'm jumpy as a cat.
Marcus's hand
holds mine tight.

     "Praying?" he asks.

"You know it," I say.

     He smiles. Cocoa eyes crinkle.
     "They'll love you–
     just don't mention religion."

I nod. There's a horde of bees
swarming in my belly
but the roots of my hair
don't tingle.

We're barely on the step
and the screen door flies open.

     "Welcome!" His moms
     are framed in the door.

I almost fall over.

One of 'em's
my English professor.

You never think of your teacher
having a life outside of school.

All four of us exclaim over this
small, small world.

Then we go in,
sit down.
They offer me wine,
I take iced tea.

It feels good
being with someone
who wants to introduce me
to his family.

And it feels even better
that I'm mostly nervous
because we all know
I have a paper due
that I should be home working on.

Just feels a normal
kind of nervous.

One I could get used to.

I Keep Messing Up

Calling one of his moms
Dr. Wolski.

> "It's Kathleen, here, Angel,"
> she says. His other mom,
> Dorothy, nods.

> "Trust me, she gets enough of
> that at school-she'd be
> insufferable if we
> kept it up at home!"

We laugh and talk
through dinner and into the night.
Turns out Dorothy is an administrator
at the hospital-and she's on something
called an ethics panel.

> "Angel has an ethical dilemma,"
> Marcus says, grabbing another
> homemade cookie off the plate.
> "Tell them about Brendan."

So I tell 'em about the broken window
and blue envelopes,
and I'm trying not to get worked up
but it's hard.

"You should absolutely
call the authorities," Dorothy
says. And she takes a sip of wine.

Kathleen shakes her head.

"I couldn't disagree more."

"Why?" Dorothy asks.

"For one thing, the money he
sends is a clear sign of remorse-
he *is* paying his debt.

"For another, Angel doesn't know
why he broke the window-that
should inform any decision she
makes." Kathleen says to me,
"You should try to find out."

Dorothy doesn't like that.

"The reason doesn't matter-
actions have consequences."

And they're off into
a philosophical argument
about crime and the meaning
of punishment.
Disagreeing but not fighting.

It's interesting to hear and
I'm trying to follow them
but it's getting late and
I accidentally yawn.
Marcus takes my hand.

"Now we've done it,"
he pretends to whisper.
"They'll be up
half the night debating . . .
Let's go."

They stop
long enough
to walk us
to the door.

"It was wonderful to meet you,"
Dorothy says. Kathleen smiles.
"See you in class."

And on the way home
even though I don't
mention religion
I'm thanking God.

You think meeting
your boyfriend's parents
for the first time
is nerve-racking?

Girl, you just try doing it trans.

(Vanessa)

Weigh-In for Wrestling Finals
at 6 a.m. Afterward
the team goes out for pancakes
before the first match at eight.

I slump at the end of the table
next to Sheahan,
across from
Flannigan.

There's a rowdiness down at the
other end, but for once Flannigan's
not in the thick of it.

I watch brown maple syrup
seep into the golden stack.

     "Nervous?" Sheahan asks.

Shake my head no.

     "Awww, she's probably
     missing her boyfriend,"
     Flannigan says,
     but not in a mean way.

I almost start crying.
It's the truth.

"We broke up."

> " 'Cause he's a fag?" Flannigan asks
> like he's genuinely curious.

I look up from the table
to see Sheahan give him a dirty look.

> "Shut up, Flannigan," he says.

We finish eating in silence.
On the way back to the tournament
Sheahan walks with me.

He's nervous,
talking a lot like he
always does before a match.

> "You know Flannigan's just a dick."

I nod.

> "I know what they say
> about Brendan, but
> I like him.
> Not like THAT,"
> he adds in a hurry.

I smile.
We walk, comfortable.

"It's so weird,
how things change,
isn't it?"

"What do you mean?"

"Like, you think you're going to be with
someone for a long time—it's October
and you ask her to the prom—or even
talk about summer plans. By the time
those roll around you're just not into each
other anymore. And I always wonder . . .
What changed? And how?"

Forty-Five Minutes Later

I'm stepping
onto the mat for my first bout and

What changed?
is the clang in my ears.

It rings even as I shoot fast,
get the takedown points

drive my chin
into the guy from Clark's shoulder

cross face,
guillotine

let him up
take him down again

and again
double cobra.

Win
because my opponent
was a bad wrestler
not because I was
on my game.

What changed?

It's what I'm still thinking when
I lose the next two matches.

Pinned both times.

In the first round.

I walk off the mat
and someone says,

> "That's what you get,
> little-girl loser."

But I barely hear it.

What Really Has Changed?

I wonder, and I'm dazed.

Disappointed in my losses,
but not surprised—
I wrestled poorly.

Waking up
to the fact that
he's not the one
who's changed
took away my focus.

Sweet Brendan
loving Brendan
Mr. Hilarious Brendan
driven Brendan
playful Brendan

even distant Brendan
and for sure
depressed Brendan

is just Brendan.

Phase or not.

Monday Morning Announcements
and the whole school gets to hear
that Miller Prep lost finals by six points.

Just so happens that's the exact number
a team forfeits
when there's a hole in the lineup.

I come out of a bathroom stall and
Rudy and Gil are waiting for me.

> "We lost because of you,
> you little faggot."

They're between me and the door.
It's class change—
outside the hallway is loud.

If I shout would anyone hear?

Blood cracks in my veins.
My heart freezes.

Or would the rest of the team
come in, hold me down?

Gil steps forward.
Rudy smiles an evil smile.

"We're gonna make you sorry
you got up this morning."

"Hell"—Gil's smiling, too—
"we're gonna make you
sorry you were born."

He steps in front of me.
Rudy's still blocking the door.

I can't move.

When the fist comes
it doubles me over
pain sears my gut
I can't breathe.

The fist comes again
only this time it connects
with my nose and I see stars.

Then I'm on my side
and Gil is kicking me
and in the distance
like some psycho sound track
I can hear Rudy laughing.

Then the door opens.
The kicking stops.

"Dudes, what's going on?"
It's Andy.

"Teaching the fag a lesson."
Gil's already stepping back.

I look over, see Andy nod.

He's the only kid
in the school
as big as Gil.
As tough.

"That's probably enough,"
he says.

"Bell's about to ring
anyway," Rudy says.

Gil heads for the exit.
When he's safely past Andy
he says, "We'll leave your
girlfriend alone."

He and Rudy laugh out the door.

I shift
to sit.

I'm slow.
I'm hurt.
I'm grateful.

I need a hand

to stand up.

Extend mine

to

Andy.

He looks at it.

Looks at me.

And shoves out the door.

I Leave School Without a Pass

The bus home
smells bad and
it wheezes and grunts;
like it's not gonna lie —
grinding away from the curb
takes effort; you'll *f i n d*
out just how hard moving
forward is. Maybe there's something
at the end of the line —
maybe there's nothing at all.
I've never been there
and for all I know, *m y*
ride's an infinite one.
Buildings and cars sliding by,
without end? What if there
was some *w a y*
to find out.
If I stayed on the bus, just
rode beyond the
horizon, checked *o u t*
of life here?
Would I find anything
at all? Angelic white forms
floating, soothing songs *o f*
joy and forgiveness?
Malicious horned beasts
with pitchforks and tails?
We used to go to church,

and yet *t h i s*
seems unlikely to me.

What I think
best case
would be,
a blank
dark room
at the end
of the line.
Dreamless sleep.

Male, female consciousness
gone to the grave
along with your *b o d y.*

No One at Home

Walking
up
stairs
is such
an effort.
I fall
into bed
for the rest
of the day
drowsing
in and out.

Don't Do Sadness

Don't do sadness
don't do sadness
don't sadness
dadness
deadness
drift
down
sad
sorry
wrong.

Wrong flesh
wrong bones
wrong
wrong
wrong
wrong

the word "wrong"
sounds wrong.

Consciousness
        sᴜrges
retreats

Little hands
grab,
poke.

Grabbing.

Poking.
"Brendy? Brendy?
Where do you hurt?"

Then shoving.

"Where do you hurt, Brendy?"

A small voice
panicked
wakes me up.

It must be late
if Courtney's home
from after-school
day care already.

"I'm okay,"
I tell her.

But I'm not.

        "Are you sick?"

"Uh-huh."

        "Did you throw up?"

"Yes," I lie.

It's the best way I know
to get everyone to
leave me alone.

But not Courtney.

> "Should I get Mommy?"

"No—I just need rest."

> "I'll read to you." She puts her face
> close to mine, repeats what
> someone's said to her for sure.

> "It's very restful."

I don't have the energy
to tell her no.

She bounces off
to get a book
and I drowse.

She brings back several,
pretends to read.

For a long time.

I fall asleep during *The Three Little Pigs*,
wake up during *Beauty and the Beast*.

    "But Beauty wasn't scared even
    though she had a scaredy face.
    She was just sad for Beast
    because he threw up."

    A kiss on my shoulder.

Eyes tight,
I wait for her to go away.

When I open them Court's gone
but Mom's there
thirty feet tall.
        "Dinnertime.
        Are you okay?"

"Not hungry," I tell her.
"Maybe something I ate."

She starts to step forward—I
think she's going
to kiss my forehead
like she did
tucking me into bed
when I was little
and I'm surprised to realize

I wouldn't mind that
right now.

Would welcome it.

The Interloper
calls her name.
She shakes her head.

    "I'll check in on you later."

Leaves.

From Sucky to Worse
The crowning touch
of the whole day,
one that would prove
God hated me—
if I believed in Him—

is when I turn on my Mac.

An e-mail from a school that starts,
We are happy to inform you,

is really saying,
You're special.
We want you!
Come be one of us.
You can ditch
your parents
your sucky town
your shitty life.

An e-mail that starts,
We regret to inform you,

is really saying,
You are a loser
with nothing to offer.
You are worthless and
we don't want you here.
You're stuck where you are,
you immoral freak of nature.

Guess which one
the University of Chicago sent?

And my pathetic first thought
is to find my phone,
call Vanessa,
tell her
about my rejection

but she knows about me

hates me.

I'm Tired

So tired of
everything.

Of pushing
that word
down.

Away.

That I AM in the
wrong body and
no one will
ever love me.

That I'm in the wrong skin
but there's no way
to make it right
because I'm not into
long fingernails,
high heels, or skirts
either.

I'm Freakboy and
there will never
be a place for me.

Anywhere.

And out of
thoughts that've
floated for
a long time

a plan starts
to take shape in
my exhausted head.

I Have My First Fight
with Marcus

heading home from

the Bean Scene

full on mochas
and conversation
about his moms.

"They're pretty great," I tell him.
He smiles.

>"I know—they liked you, too—
>even if you told them
>the wrong dilemma."

"Huh?"

>"I thought you were going to ask
>them about the ethics of a
>friendship with a client."

"It's not about me—
it's what I should do
about Brendan breaking
the window!"

"The window thing is
Brendan's," he agrees.
"But you said yourself
you'd have a hard time
explaining your friendship
to Dr. Martina,
because he came to Willows
as a potential client."

His words poke
at me and, Girl,
I stop walking.

"You're keeping something
from your boss because you think
it might show you did wrong.
Baby, that's an ethical dilemma
right there."

"You sayin' I'm wrong
to be friends with
a kid who needs one?"

I stare him right
in his cocoa eyes.

"Easy there!"
He takes a step back.
"No judgment, it was just
an observation!"

The hell?!!

Sounded
pretty judgmental
to me.

I look away, try not to notice how his
biceps bulge when he crosses his arms.

I'm ready to
tell him
he sounds like a
self-righteous asshole
when he

    says soft, "I'm not even saying
    it's for sure wrong–I'm just
    saying maybe you should give
    Dr. Martina a chance
    to weigh in on it."

My Boyfriend Won

our first fight because, Lord?
I think he's right.

But I'm gonna need
Your help in this
for sure.

Confession is good for the soul
but it might be
hell on a résumé.

Marcus kisses me good night
when we get to my place.
And even though
there's no answer when I call

I leave a message for Brendan
before I go to sleep.

Because if I'm risking
getting in trouble
at my job,
I may as well be
a true friend–

and pay it forward first.

Angel's Message
A beacon
over water,

> "I'm not gonna lie—
> I'm mad—but
> I didn't give you
> a chance to explain.
> I wanna
> know more.
> Give me a call
> so we can talk."

Shines useless

on a

sinking ship.

Asking Myself the Biggest Question

Pills or rope?
Gets interrupted
by Courtney,
who comes
to my door.
It's late
she should
be in bed.

"Brendy? I brought you a cookie!"

She hands me a snickerdoodle,
props the Max doll I gave her for Christmas
on my nightstand,
settles her back against me.

"I made it for you. Eat it!"
she demands.

Long after you go down
and the vessel rusts apart

your bones sunken
buried in the ocean floor

I wonder if you miss people?

Lillian Bruner's Having a Party
I go with Sheahan.

None of us are strangers to big houses
but Lillian's is gargantuan.

And I want to make a joke about her
needing it to house her giant ego

but Sheahan has a crush
on her and I don't want anyone
to think I'm a snide bitch.

No one here knows me well enough
to know that a joke is just a joke.

I miss Julie
I miss Tanya
I miss Brendan.
The people who know me.

The music's crazy loud
so we wander out
to the backyard

drink beer
from red plastic cups
stand away from the smokers

watch a couple of seniors
play some weird
gladiator game on the lawn.

Andy runs out of the house,
tackles one of the players.
"Centurion, welcome!"
the other one shouts.

"Talked to Brendan lately?"
Sheahan asks me.

I shake my head.

"Sucks to be him."

We watch the guys
rolling around on the grass
being stupid.

And all I can think
is how much it DOES suck.

Because if I'm feeling
friendless even with Sheahan,

Brendan really is
                    alone.
We never had that
we'll-still-be-friends talk.

It Sucks Even More

that I'm good at things

as challenging
as ceramics

as grueling
as wrestling

but simple friendship
turned out to be
something too hard
for me
to stick with.

(BRENDAN)

Sunday Night Dinner
I'm not hungry
but it's my turn to set the table.

Courtney's happy—
she gets to light the candles,
but wrinkles her nose.

        "Brendy, you stink."

"So do you."

        "No really." Mom butts in.
        "When was the last time
        you showered?"

"Really?"

I can't say exactly
when the last time
my skin, this skin
was clean.

        "Really," she says, glancing at
        the Interloper. "Dinner's not
        for twenty minutes.
        Go. Bathe."

She manages to look disgusted
and concerned
at the same time.

A half hour later
I'm clean and
at the table and

exhausted.

Eating's a chore.

After Dinner

I go lie down.

Mom comes into
my room, sits
on the bed.

My eyes stay closed.
She doesn't beat
around the bush.

"Honey, I'm worried about you."

Her hand smooths
my high forehead.

"I'm okay,
just don't feel well."

"I hear that a lot from you."

"It's true."

"Even so—I have a thought . . ."

Uncertainty in her voice
makes me open my eyes.

Hers are welling.
There's Courtney in her face.

"I know you're not comfortable
talking to me—
and I know I've had issues
with counseling in the past . . ."

"Why?" I ask.

She gets a faraway look.

It lasts a long time

and I think she's forgotten
the question, until she
speaks again.
"I think I misread your father's
intentions," she says quietly.

"When people divorce, even when
they try to keep it amicable . . .
there's a lot of hurt feelings,
misunderstanding . . ."

She looks down at me
and I want to look away
but I don't.

"Now I think he really was
worried about you."
She stares
off again.

I stay silent.

Finally:
"But maybe Dr. Andrews
just isn't a good fit?"

The whole conversation
so out of left field.
No idea what to say.

"I just want you to know our
insurance has a list
of other therapists,
if you want,
and if it's something you choose
for yourself—maybe it
could be a good thing."

I'm tired.
She's trying.
She's too late.

"Andrews is fine.
I'm just sick."

"Maybe—but it might be good
for you to talk to someone else,
anyway . . . Will you?"

I'm not going to argue
but I'm not committing either.
"We'll see."

She doesn't push
for more than that.

The truth is

I am not planning to talk to anyone else

ever.

Tiny White Torpedoes

squeezed tight in my fist.
Leftovers from breast surgery.

Discovered behind the vitamins
in Mom's medicine cabinet.

How many,
I wonder?

How many
would take me under
slow
breath
heartbeat

let
this
body
this
wrong
body

this
brain
this
wrong
brain

sleep?

No Note
could ever explain
and why
reveal
that the
inexplicable
even exists

when it will just
lead to more
questions?

No answers.

Far beyond
feeling mean
at the thought
of making them guess

all I feel
is a forever
dull ache

that will
probably
exist

for as
long as
I do.

Midnight

The wedge of light
under Mom's door
is snuffed out.

I line up the pills
on my nightstand

one row of twenty

is this it?

rearrange them
two rows of ten

I don't *think* it will hurt

now three of six
with two left over

and even if it does—

now four of five
with none left over—

it'll stop eventually

now two of seven
with six left over

No school tomorrow;
they'll let me sleep

now two of eight
with four left over

hours from now
I don't know where I'll be—

now two of nine
with two left over—

but this body will be here

stiff,
cold?

      "BRENDY!!!"
      My door slams open
      a hallway shriek,
      night-terror eyes wild
      hair sticking out.

My heart explodes
like it did
that night
in the graveyard.

Courtney's too freaked
by whatever monster
she's seen

to notice my girlish yell

      or the pills
      on my nightstand.

I'm Leading Her

back to her room
when Mom sticks
her head out.

"Nightmare," I say.
"I've got it."

       "Are you sure?" She yawns,
       clearly hoping to go back to bed.

My throat closes; that's it.
I *will* be Little Mother.

In the pretty pink
princess palace.

I sit with my baby sister
waiting for her to sleep,

heart squeezing,
folding, turning over.

Courtney
could be the one
to find me dead.

What would that do?

What would
her tomorrow look like?

And the tomorrows
after that?

How messed up
would she be?

The little-kid
memory
of touching
poking
prodding

my lifeless body?

Not Dying
isn't the same as
choosing to live,

not right away.

In the bathroom
I pee sitting down,
thinking about it.

Go to the beach?
Would the *i m p u l s e*
to throw my body into
night-blackened water
outlast my bio-instinct
to breathe?

Would this body struggle
against my own intention
mind, soul, body connection *d e n i e d*?

Would I care who
found me, looking like
a bloated small seal,
a tuskless walrus?
As long as it wasn't Courtney?

What do humpbacks think
when they beach themselves
on land and people go to crazy efforts,
tugging them
pushing them

rolling them
back into the sea?

Afterward, do the whales
look back to shore, thinking,
I feel better now—
and there are
some humans
I need to   t h a n k
for disallowing my
self-destruction.

Or do they just
think, *Oh,   G o d,*
I have to try, try again.

When I get into bed
I think maybe
I won't try

not right now anyway.

Instead
I call Angel
first thing in the morning

because
there has to be
a better way
to deal
with being me

and that
other option
will always
exist

if I need it.

We Meet Down at Mono Cove

Waves crash
sea spray
and
I come out
into sunshine
that almost hurts
my eyes.

We walk.
I talk.
Angel listens.

I tell her about that night.

"I don't know why I did it."

And I don't, not for sure.

"Maybe I thought
the sound of breaking glass
would drown out
that word?"

She nods.

      "Uncool," she says.
      "But I think I understand."
Pauses.

"You got freaked
figuring out
you're genderqueer."

And even though
Angel says it quiet
the new word
bounces off the bluff
soft round sound
for such sharp edges.

Queerbait.

Queer as a three-dollar bill.

Smear the queer.

I consider
in silence.

Genderqueer.

The way
she says it
doesn't feel
like a put-down.

I slip it on over my head
stretch around
feel it on my skin

                    not male

          not female.

A gull wheels by,
swoops down,
pecks in the
tangled
seaweed.

It reminds me of
the grabby women
at the bra-and-panty table
in Girl World.

"I have no idea where I fit in."

          She smiles. "You think
          you're the only one?"

"I'm just not . . . flamboyant."

          "Shit, it's not about
          how you dress—it's
          not even about your body parts.
          Uh-uh—it's about your soul."

Maybe, maybe not.

My voice
is small in my ears.
"I'll feel like Freakboy
no matter where I go."

She stops walking,
looks me in the eye.

> "Everyone feels like a freak
> until they make up their mind
> they're not."

It's full confession time.

"I read about people who've known
forever they belong in a different body,

"but I'm not even always sure I'm trans.

"Sometimes, being a guy is . . . not horrible."

My shrug tightens,
my shoulders go round.

"Sometimes, it hurts more than anything."

A   tortuous
back   and   forth.

"What's it even mean
that I'm never sure
either way?"

And really.

How can
you ever
get a grip
on THAT?

        "Lord knows,
        we don't need
        more labels," she says.

But then

she gives me

two words

that push
        the
                pieces
of
        the

puzzle together.

"Gender Fluid"

I study the phrase.

My soul a vapor
            wafting
                wafting
between male
and female.

I am
      everything
      and
      nothing

      but moist breath and soul.

We sit in the sand
backs against
the bluff
quiet
for a moment
just watching the waves

until a couple
      one man
      one woman
walk by us,
holding hands,
at ease.

Vapor condenses
falls to earth. Heavy.

"I just can't imagine what
my future could possibly look like."

        "Only God knows what's in store!
        You could win the lottery or
        get hit by a bus."

In spite of me
I almost smile.
"I'd rather win the lottery."

            "Only one thing's for sure,"
            she says. "You will never,
            EVER
            beat me
            at Mordock's Giant."

And now I do smile.

A small thing
that feels good.

(Vanessa)

Teacher In-Service Day
means no school
but Brendan's not home.

     "Would you like to come in though?"
     his mom asks me.

She gestures on a cloud
of light perfume that
Grand-maman would appreciate.

I think of the way
Mrs. Chase traded in
one husband for another
and I realize
that Grand-maman's little lessons
are all about how to get a guy
but not about how to have a relationship
with anyone.

Even yourself.

Waiting Around

is not what I do best,
but I think
about Brendan
all alone.

He needs a friend.

I need a friend.

It's worth some time
with his mom.

Everything looks like
it did weeks ago.

I sit on the same old sofa—
she offers the same old soda.
                    "We've missed you,"
                    she says.

The same old grandfather clock
ticks away the awkward minutes

but it all somehow feels different.

"I've been busy with
wrestling."

                    "Oh, of course! I'm just
                    glad to see you.
                    Brendan's seemed a little
                    down lately."

She's looking at me
with some expectation
in her eyes, like I can
tell her what's going on with him.
But I can't.
And I'm feeling weirded out,
so I make small talk
until I can politely leave.

At the door,
she surprises me
with a hug.

"I'm glad you came by—
Brendan needs his friends."

I head to my car
thinking that
of all the things
I'm good at,
wrestling,
ceramics,
even school,

being a friend
is not what I do best.

Not to Brendan.
Not to Julie.
Not to Tanya.

But I'm willing
to work on it.

With all of them.

(Angel)

We Go Back to Brendan's
and his girlfriend's
just comin' down the walk.
He seems surprised to see her.

>"Vanessa!"
>We just stand there
>looking at each other,
>till he remembers his manners.

>"This is Angel."

>We shake hands
>like we're old people.

>"Courtney's new babysitter?"
>Her voice has an edge to it.

Brendan looks to me
for a second
like he wants to lie
but he straightens his shoulders.

>"I'm sorry, no."

She nods once
turns to get in the car.

Brendan's face is so sad . . .
these two need to talk.

I was supposed to go in with him
get a game he was tellin' me about
but it can wait.

"I better get going.
I have a big date
with my boyfriend, Marcus," I say.

Brendan's look,
pure gratitude
sunshine.

I Take the Bus to Willows

My heart starts beating
when I see Dr. M's in her office.

"You got a minute?" I ask.
She smiles, gestures me in.

It's warm today
and her blazer's slung
on the back of the chair. Even so,
she looks totally professional.

Someone you can look up to.

"I have an ethical dilemma," I say,
and she raises her eyebrows.

I tell her about
the first time I met Brendan
when he got sick in the planter.

And she looks serious
when I tell her about how
he came into Willows
a few weeks later,
how I didn't think he'd come back,
and how I gave him my number again.

I tell her about going to his house,
borrowing his PS2.
I tell her about everything
except the window

because Brendan's
paying for it
and I've pretty much
decided it's
his to tell.
I'm hoping
one day
he just might.

When I've finished talking
she leans back in her chair,
still looking serious.

> "The fact that he
> technically wasn't a client
> does make this a gray area."

"Uh-huh."

> "But you're correct
> in thinking that there's an
> ethical problem here," she says.

And my heart sinks.

> "There are good reasons
> for the no-fraternization policy.
> Our kids can be fragile—
> an unscrupulous person
> could take advantage."

Dr. M's chair creaks
when she leans toward me.

"But I know you, Angel.

"You're not unscrupulous
just unschooled. The fact you
brought this to my attention
tells me you've learned enough
that it won't happen again."

"It won't," I promise,
breathing easier.

"Your heart
is in the right place." She smiles.

"And I'm dead sure
that from now on,
your boundaries

will be, too."

"The Truth Will Set You Free"

Glad I figured that out.
Glad Brendan did, too . . .

but there's such a thing
as too free.

I gotta remember
to give him a call-tell him
to think long and hard
before he comes out to his mom
and Claude the Interloper

unless he's in a position
to pay for school himself.

Not easy to be trans
but I KNOW

it's gonna be easier
with a college degree.

I can't settle Brendan's confusion
for him-no one can

but I told him he might wanna
look for a therapist
trained in gender issues.

Not to "cure" him
just to help figure things out.

And I can help, too,
that's an Angel's job.

When I leave Willows,
Marcus is out front
waiting for me

a smile on his face,
kick-ass
Bean Scene mocha
for me
in his hand.

> "Thought we could
> walk to the park."

Thank you, God,
for everything.

Angel Takes Off

Vanessa's still here.
It's awkward.
Standing
close enough
to touch
but not
speaking.

An airplane buzzes overhead.
I look up to see the vapor trail.

"Angel is trans," I finally say.

I don't know
if that's an okay thing
outing her like that.
It's all so complicated.

I just thought it might
make a difference to Vanessa.

She says nothing.

"Want to come in?"

      "You want to be like that?"

Her face
is angled away
hard to read.
I want to touch it.

      "You want to look like that?"

"I don't know."

This time nothing breaks
the silence.

She turns to me.
Her eyes serious, dark,
and I can't see myself
in them.

      Finally: "Did you love me?"

"I still love you," I say.

      "But you want to be a girl."

Her voice flat,
not accusing
just stating.

"It's complicated,"
I tell her.

She nods like she understands
but I don't think she does.

"Maybe I'm a lesbian," I say,
and it falls,
a too-soon joke.

A wisp of her hair
is coming loose
from her ponytail

my hand twitches
to touch it,
to touch her.

      Sadly, slowly.
      "But I'm not," she says.

Understanding that
makes it no less painful.
She was mine
and now she isn't.

I think there's nothing left to say
till she leans forward
      kisses me on the cheek.

      "But I
      will always
      love you."

After she leaves
I go into the house,
find my mom
in the music room.

She's sitting at the harp
not playing,
just staring
off into space.

I wonder
what she's thinking.

I'll probably never know.

She looks up,
realizes I'm standing there
staring at her.

>   "Everything okay?" she asks.
>   Her voice hopeful
>   for a second,
>   young.

I nod.

"I'd like to go see someone
other than Dr. Andrews."

No

    mo-

      ment

        of *Aha!*

         I'll just

         go have

         surgery and

         that will make

         it all better. And

         definitely no *Aha!*

         I'm in just the right

         body, I'll   leave it

There Is   as it is.   My fu-

No Tidy Ending   ture is   murky

for Someone   and some   days are

Like Me   more femme   than the

       others but today, on this day,

       and in this moment, I can

       live with that.

Acknowledgments

So many people helped me with this project, from answering nosy questions to pointing me in the direction of resources to loving and supporting me while I wrote.

My heartfelt apologies if I've inadvertently left anyone out.

First, I want to thank my amazing editor, Joy Peskin, for her patience, enthusiasm, and keen instincts. The book you hold in your hands is vastly better than it started out to be thanks to her loving ministrations.

Much adoration and appreciation goes to my loving and supportive family, both immediate and extended. Having a writer in the house can be kind of torturous—I'm grateful you are up to the challenge. Thank you to Steve, especially, for being such an excellent sounding board. Your insightful suggestions helped immensely.

Huge thanks go to my earliest readers, Kathleen Wolski, Damen Cook (the video game consultation was much appreciated!), Kelly Sheahan, Susan Hart Lindquist, Jim Averbeck, Lyn Wyman, Andrea Bechert, Kevin McCaughey, and Michele Veillon. Thanks also to my writing tribe and team members, including my fabulous agent, Tracey Adams, and, of course, Kim Turrisi and SCBWI—who got the ball rolling in the first place! To Lee Wind for informing a key moment near the book's conclusion. Thank you to all of the real-life Brendans and Angels who were willing to openly and honestly talk to me, and a huge thanks to Anthony Ross and the fine folk at Outlet in Mountain View, California. Finally, a very special thank-you needs to go to Ellen Hopkins, who, when I went to her, wringing my hands and whining that she needed to write something for gender-variant kids, listened patiently, then said, "No, this is a story you need to write yourself."

My cup of gratitude runneth over.

Resources

Trevor Lifeline: 1-866-488-7386
thetrevorproject.org
Providing crisis intervention to LGBTQ youth

lgbtcenters.org/Centers/find-a-center.aspx
International database of LGBTQ centers

imatyfa.org
Assisting families with trans and gender-variant youth

community.pflag.org
For parents, families, and friends of LGBTQ individuals (also links to TNET, their transgender network)

genderspectrum.org
Providing support and education

genderfork.com
A supportive community for the expression of identities across the gender spectrum

gsanetwork.org
Gay Straight Alliance

projectoutlet.org
LGBTQ support and education in Mountain View, California

glbtnationalhelpcenter.org
Serving the LGBTQ community nationally

plannedparenthood.org
Addressing LGBTQ health

leewind.org
I'm Here. I'm Queer. What the Hell Do I Read?

FURTHER READING

This list is nonfiction, but there are some noteworthy novels and even a couple of picture books that bring greater understanding to this topic. Check out Lee Wind's great blog, leewind.org, for a huge list of LGBTQ titles.

Feeling Wrong in Your Own Body: Understanding What It Means to Be Transgender, Jaime A. Seba

The Full Spectrum: A New Generation of Writing About Gay, Lesbian, Bisexual, Transgender, Questioning and Other Identities, edited by David Levithan and Billy Merrell

GLBTQ: The Survival Guide for Gay, Lesbian, Bisexual, Transgender, and Questioning Teens, Kelly Huegel

The Riddle of Gender: Science, Activism, and Transgender Rights, Deborah Rudacille

She's Not There: A Life in Two Genders, Jennifer Finney Boylan

The Transgender Child: A Handbook for Families and Professionals, Stephanie A. Brill and Rachel Pepper

Transgender Explained for Those Who Are Not, Joanne Herman

Transgender Warriors: Making History from Joan of Arc to Dennis Rodman, Leslie Feinberg

Transparent: Love, Family, and Living the T with Transgender Teenagers, Cris Beam

GOFISH

KRISTIN ELIZABETH CLARK

What did you want to be when you grew up?
Between the ages of about five to nine I wanted to be Peter Pan because I really, really wanted to fly.

When did you realize you wanted to be a writer?
When I was nine, a writer visited our school. By then I'd become an avid reader. As my Peter Pan career fell by the wayside, I decided that writing was it for me. I could shoot for a metaphor here and say that writing is like flying, the dazzling highs, etc., etc., etc.—but I'm not going to.

What's your favorite childhood memory?
My favorite childhood memory is also one of my first. (Which might just mean it was all downhill from there.) I wasn't yet three, and we still lived in Ohio. In the summer, the days were super long, and the sun was always still up when I was put to bed. One night I climbed out of my crib and escaped from the house at twilight. Outside, magical sparks of light zigged and zagged through the air—I'd never been awake to see fireflies before. I sat on the porch in the warmth and deepening dusk, mesmerized. The sense memory of the joy and awe I felt at sharing the world with such creatures remains with me to this day.

What was your favorite thing about school?
I really disliked school. All the math and science and social studies and even recess interfered with my precious reading time.

What were your hobbies as a kid? What are your hobbies now?
Obviously, reading was huge for me, but so was theater. It's the same today.

What sparked your imagination for *Freakboy*?
My child came out to me as gender fluid. I've gone into detail elsewhere about this, but she really inspired me, and then stood over my shoulder as I wrote it. However, I'm always careful to point out that while she was the inspiration, the book itself is fiction.

What's the best advice you have ever received about writing?
That nearly every first draft is crappy, so don't be alarmed by what you see on the page. Revision is a beautiful thing.

What advice do you wish someone had given you when you were younger?
That the embarrassing thing you think you just said or did will stay with you longer than it will with anyone else. Whatever it was will recede in importance and memory for others while you're still squirming. Get over it. This too shall pass.

Did you ever get writer's block? What did you do to get back on track?
As a matter of fact, yes. After I finished *Freakboy*, I had a terrible block. I put a lot of pressure on myself because *Freakboy*

had been so well received, and I was sure that whatever came next would be a disappointment. I kept starting projects and then abandoning them because my writing wasn't perfect. I'm fortunate that my wise and wonderful editor, Joy Peskin, gave me the time and space I needed to figure it out, because I tussled with the block for what seemed like a long time. I questioned whether I'd ever tell another story. Every time I sat down to write, what came out on the page was awful. I began avoiding my computer like it was covered in poison oak. I felt like such a loser. This went on for months. I was really anxious about it all and the only thing that kind of helped was taking these long, solitary walks. One night after taking such a walk, I was drowsing off to sleep when I had an epiphany: A draft of an imperfect book would better than no book at all. That simple thought freed me up, and the next morning I was able to write again.

What do you want readers to remember about your books?

I'd like my books to be remembered as empathy gyms, where readers were able to strengthen the muscles of their compassion. It's hard to mock or bully or marginalize someone once you've walked a mile in their shoes.

Tell us about your next book.

I'm really excited about it. It's called *Jess, Chunk, and the Road Trip to Infinity*. Even though the characters are different, it's not in verse, and it's told in a much lighter tone, I think of it as a philosophical sequel to *Freakboy*. In *Freakboy*, Brendan is exploring and grappling with what it means to be trans, and that's the issue. In *Jess and Chunk*, Jess just happens to be trans. It's an important part of the story certainly, but the book's focused more on issues having to do with her relationship with her estranged father and her shifting feelings about her best friend.

I also love that it features a road trip—as far as I'm concerned, there's nothing better than a road trip with good friends.

A funny new novel about
friendship, identity, and family.

Keep reading for an excerpt.

CHAPTER 1

Something about my mom's New Age music makes me want to stab myself in the eye. Although anatomically speaking, the ear might be a better area to stab if I'm serious about not having to listen to it anymore. The sound is coming from the living room and our house is so small there's no escaping it.

I'm in my bedroom packing to the backdrop of a thrumming harp and the low hollow shriek of a bamboo flute. Underneath that there's the *shhhhht* of the *Vogue* magazine sliding into my laptop case, and the *snick* of a Viva La Juicy perfume bottle hitting my straight-edge razor. It's five days after high school graduation, I'm packing for my first parent-free road trip, and I can almost hear my old life and my new one clinking against each other.

I add a couple of button-down shirts and some girl jeans to the Space Camp duffel bag I've had since seventh grade.

I'm definitely going to need new luggage before I head off to college in August.

Wallet, check.

Sweatshirt, check.

Sketchbook, check.

Mom comes in and hands me a tube of sunscreen.

"I have some." I open my bag a little wider so she can see.

"That's only SPF fifty," she says. "This is seventy."

I sigh and take the seventy.

"No skin cancer for you!" she says in a weird accent. I know it's a reference to some comedy skit about soup or something, but I'm damned if I know what's funny about it.

"Just want you to be safe," she says in her normal voice. Her urge to protect me can be irritating, but just now I'm heading halfway across the country—San Jose to Chicago without her—and in this case her concern might be warranted.

I look at her and smile.

Her hair used to be straight like mine, but five years ago she had cancer, and after remission her hair grew back soft and wavy. She calls it the chemo curl.

Even with different hair, people say we look a lot alike. Same blue eyes, same noses, and now that I'm taking hormones, I swear our jawlines are becoming similar too.

It's not that I want us to dress in matching outfits or anything, but when you're transitioning, there are worse things than realizing you look like your mom. Especially if your mom is as beautiful as mine used to be.

"You're wearing that?" she asks, indicating the thin white Power Puff Girls T-shirt I slept in last night. Earlier than expected results from hormones are in evidence. (Yay, breasts!)

I point to a thicker T-shirt and the light blue hoodie lying on my bed.

I've been taking hormones for seven months now, since November 22, the day I turned eighteen, and I'm kind of at an in-between-looking place at this point.

People who know me see what they expect to see, what they think they've seen all along. A sort of skinny guy with a shortish body and longish hair. But under a thin shirt it's obvious that breasts are growing.

I'm friendly with a few kids from my art classes and theater, but I'm not tight with any of them, so my mom and my best friend Chunk are the only ones who (privately) use the right pronouns and call me by my new name (Jess). They're also the only ones who know about my (I'm gonna go ahead and say it) new development.

I toss a pair of nondescript jeans on top of the thick T-shirt and hoodie mix on the bed. Mom nods, satisfied that I'm not putting myself in danger by flaunting my sexy lady body at a time when rigorous shaving is still necessary, and turns to leave. "Breakfast in five."

The clock says 8:30.

"I need to finish packing so we can get on the road!"

"You're in a hurry for someone who originally didn't want to go," she says over her shoulder.

I'm an expert at decoding my mom's voice; her tone is singsongy, teasing, and not malicious at all.

"You're right," I agree.

I haven't spoken to my dad in more than a year, since he'd

refused to cosign a waiver that would have allowed me to get hormones before I was eighteen. The fact that it ultimately worked out okay in terms of timing—I was graduating high school identifying as a boy and starting college identifying as a girl—didn't make me any less bitter about having my gender dysphoria dismissed as a phase.

Six weeks ago, when the invitation to his wedding showed up, my mom opened it. ("I wanted to see if it was what I thought it was, so we could talk about it" was her excuse for invading my privacy.)

I said no effing way am I going. In fact, before dropping the RSVP card in the mail, I practically scratched a hole in the paper over the box marked *Regrets* and then wrote the word *no* over it, just to make sure my father and his cow of a fiancée got my point.

I'm not going to your wedding and I'm not sorry.

Bizarrely enough, my mom thought I should go.

"Anger is a coal that burns only the person who holds it," she told me.

She's been a lunatic all my life in one way or another. Currently she's a very peaceful and New Agey one. A year and a half ago she went to a retreat for cancer survivors and came back saying things like "In Spiritual Forgiveness, there are no victims. Everything is in Divine Order," and "All is in accordance with our soul contracts."

Pretty impressive for someone whose EX-HUSBAND IS MARRYING HER FORMER BEST FRIEND.

Except for the (to me) interminable year Jan lived with her

boyfriend Roger, my mom's best friend, single and childless, spent so much time at our house we called the guest room Jan's lair. She and I hung out a ton. She bought me a sketchbook for my eighth birthday and then made Saturday morning art lessons a tradition. She'd drive me up to Big Basin State Park, just so I could sketch the redwoods because they were my favorite things to draw.

That's right. My father the transphobe is marrying a woman I called Aunt Jan for most of my life.

And my mother's "Spiritual Acceptance" is taking some getting used to.

Because really, when you've settled into a groove of hating your father it's nicer to have someone hating him right alongside you, you know?

In any case, it wasn't Mom who convinced me to travel the two thousand miles to the wedding.

It was Chunk.

– – – – – – –

"Don't forget you'll need to clean the kitchen before you leave," Mom calls from down the hall.

Some things are nonnegotiable. My cleaning the kitchen after meals is one of them. According to her (recent) philosophy, when your kitchen is in the feng shui health area of your house, tidiness is of the utmost importance.

"Then you're going to have to change the music," I call back, and turn to my closet. Next to a pair of skinny jeans, on the side of the closet I think of as the girl side, hangs the costume I designed for the character of Muzzy when our school did *Thoroughly Modern Millie* a couple of months ago.

The girl who played Muzzy and I happen to be a similar size. And it also happens that I designed a glorious garment that *somehow* fits me to a T.

Imagine that.

Besides the Muzzy dress and the skinny jeans, there are only a couple of outfits on the girl side of the closet. Two shirts with intricate designs and flowy, floaty hems and sleeves, plus a pair of wide-legged yoga pants that I got at East West, my mom's favorite hippie store.

I've only ever worn the shirts and yoga pants inside my house.

The clothes I wear in public are pretty gender-neutral: sweatshirts, boy jeans, a few button-down shirts, run-of-the-mill hoodies, paint-splattered Vans. So far, mine is a no-style style. It's kind of boring, but designed to fly under the radar. Important at Kennedy High, but not anymore.

I shiver.

There's no way the Muzzy dress will fly under any radar. It weighs a ton because the entire thing is covered in black sequins, except for the bodice, which is slashed across the front with silver bugle beads. The cut is long and narrow, with a slit up the side.

I've never shown my true self to the outside world, and yet this is what I plan to wear to my father's wedding.

Because, really, nothing says "F U, Dad" like showing up in a dress, when he used to make you wear a Cub Scout uniform.

I take the sublime, sequined concoction off the hanger and gently roll it around a pair of black satin ballet flats. My hand fumbles with the zipper when I close the duffel bag.

Am I really going to do this?